Praise for *Monsters in the Mist*

"Brimming with mystery and chilling moments, *Monsters in the Mist* is an atmospheric middle-grade novel that will captivate you from the very first page!"

—Lindsay Currie, author of
The Peculiar Incident on Shady Street, *Scritch Scratch*, and *What Lives in the Woods*

"Full of shivery atmospheric and poignant remembrances, *Monsters in the Mist* is an otherworldly tale that gently and bravely explores how to confront the very things that haunt you."

—Heather Kassner, author of *The Plentiful Darkness*

"Plenty of scares pepper this deeply haunting novel, but its true power lies in its ability to offer hope in the darkest of times."

—Ronald L. Smith, author of *Hoodoo* and *Gloomtowns*

Praise for *The Wolf of Cape Fen*

"A stunning seaside fairy tale that will absorb readers until the very end."

—*Booklist*

"An atmospheric, mysterious tale of magic, community, and the true meaning of family, *The Wolf of Cape Fen* is a gorgeous debut that will hook its readers from the first page."

—Diane Magras, author of *The Mad Wolf's Daughter*

"A mesmerizing piece of magical realism packed with mystery, suspense, and, most important, love."

—*School Library Journal*

"A hauntingly gorgeous fable full of lofty dreams, terrible bargains, and accepting who you are. Cape Fen's secrets and magic had me enthralled from the start, and the conclusion to this dark and wondrous tale will stick with me forever."

—Sean Easley, author of *The Hotel Between* series

"Intriguing mystery... Laced with dreams, this perplexing fantasy rewards persistent readers."

—*Kirkus Reviews*

"Debut author Brandt's atmospheric, genre-bending middle grade novel brings grim fairy tale magic to a small peninsular town in the early 20th century."

—*Publishers Weekly*

"Eliza's story weaves its magic around you, as wild and wondrous as the dreams at the book's heart. Cape Fen and its inhabitants will haunt you long after the book is closed!"

—Cindy Baldwin, author of
Where the Watermelons Grow and
The Stars of Whistling Ridge

"Juliana Brandt's *The Wolf of Cape Fen* is an enthralling, atmospheric tale of two sisters, their hopes and dreams, and their unwavering love amid threats of mysterious bargains and treacherous magic. It is a remarkable debut filled with haunting details and unraveling secrets that are sure to captivate readers till the very end."

—Gail D. Villanueva, author of
My Fate According to the Butterfly and *Sugar and Spite*

"Softly spangled black and white chapter title illustrations preface brief dream interludes belonging to other Fenians, emphasizing that the whole community is bound up in the baron's magic and helping to harmonize the novel's contrasting moods of coastal-town hominess and stark unease."

—*The Bulletin of the Center for Children's Books*

Praise for *A Wilder Magic*

"[Kids] expecting a big move may find comfort in Sybaline's eventual acceptance of her need to leave the valley."

—*The Bulletin of the Center for Children's Books*

"*A Wilder Magic*, with its beautiful imagery, relevant themes, and inspiring female characters, is vividly enchanting."

—*Shelf Awareness*

"I was immediately pulled in by Brandt's lyrical prose, the unique magic, and Sybaline's fear of the unknown. The author weaves a compelling story infused with a wild magic that will appeal to middle grade readers and their gatekeepers."

—Jessica Vitalis, author of *The Wolf's Curse*

"If you want your heart to ache and then heal, if you've ever been scared to step out into the unknown, if you love innovative magic systems, then keep this one on your radar."

—Lorelei Savaryn, author of
The Circus of Stolen Dreams

"*A Wilder Magic* has a dreamlike quality and deep emotional themes of dealing with change, seamlessly woven into the story of a family whose magic is tied to the valley they live in."

—Ash Van Otterloo, author of *Cattywampus* and *A Touch of Ruckus*

Also by Juliana Brandt

The Wolf of Cape Fen

A Wilder Magic

MONSTERS IN THE MIST

JULIANA BRANDT

sourcebooks
young readers

SPECTRE CRIB
LIGHTHOUSE

INGRAM
LIGHTHOUSE

ISLE
PHILIPPEAUX

SHIPYARD
LIGHTHOUSE

ISLE
PHILIPPEAUX
CEMETERY

GRAVING
LIGHTHOUSE

Published by Sourcebooks Young Readers, an imprint of Sourcebooks Kids
P.O. Box 4410, Naperville, Illinois 60567–4410
(630) 961-3900
sourcebooks.com

Cataloging-in-Publication Data is on file with the Library of Congress.

This product conforms to all applicable CPSIA standards.

Source of Production: Versa Press, East Peoria, Illinois, United States
Date of Production:March 2022
Run Number: 5024720

Printed and bound in the United States of America.
VP 10 9 8 7 6 5 4 3 2 1

DEDICATION

To Mom, for showing me the sort of love that says, *Every dream you will ever have for yourself is one I will have for you too.*

To Dad, for showing me the sort of love that says, *I will always encourage you to be exactly who you are, no part of you needs to change to suit the rest of the world.*

And to those who feel they have no voice: Some of the most important words we ever speak are the ones that are difficult and take time to find.

1

The windows of the Third Keeper's home at Graving Lighthouse quivered, restless in their frames as the wind outside crept against their edges and tried to sneak in. White fog swirled, tendrils snaking together to form two gaping holes at the center of the window. A small slit grew beneath them, almost as if a thin smile were widening beneath night-black eyes. The fog grinned at Glennon McCue.

Walking into the dining room on soft-soled shoes, Glennon's mother set down the last part of supper before him—a casserole dish with an assortment of vegetables he didn't want to eat. The scent of brussels sprouts and green beans combined with the tang of wet lake air outside. It mixed into a sickly-sweet scent that made his stomach churn.

"Lovely evening out, isn't it?" Mom poured tea for herself, placing one delicate hand atop the pot to hold the lid steady.

Glennon glanced dubiously outside the window. Fingerlings of wind clawed at the windows and rattled the glass.

"Wind sprites," Leeunah murmured beside him.

"Don't say that. Wind sprites aren't real," Glennon said. It was their dad who usually told his sister the difference between real and imaginary, but since he was overseas for work, the job was left to Glennon. Half the time he didn't know what mythology or folklore Lee referred to, but he *did* know he was supposed to remind her that magical creatures weren't real.

"I'll talk about them all I like," Lee said.

"Dad wouldn't like it."

"Dad isn't *here*."

He started to tell Lee that just because Dad wasn't there, didn't mean they shouldn't still obey him, but the stairs opposite the small dining room creaked and down the uneven steps came Uncle Job. He was a big man, with shoulders that brushed the edges of door frames when he passed through them. Up until a few months before, he'd worked at a lighthouse on the coast of Lake Superior, but a tremendous storm with massive waves had flooded the lighthouse and broken apart the flooring. That's how Uncle Job ended up on Isle Philippeaux; he'd been transferred while the lighthouse was being fixed. Harsh red lines roped up Uncle Job's right arm, scars from the injuries he'd sustained during the accident.

Uncle Job sat at the head of the table. As he did, he glanced at each of the chairs and their occupants beside him. A frown wrinkled the chapped skin between his brows. It was as if he wasn't quite sure how he'd ended up with guests in his home, even though he'd been the one to invite them.

Glennon's dad had traveled overseas for teaching fellowships loads of times before. Usually when he left, the family moved from their home in Minneapolis and into Glennon's grandmother's house. She'd passed away last year, though, and so this time, Mom had moved them north to her brother's house. Each time his dad left, the length of the trip grew. One week at first, which turned into three on the next trip. One month which turned into two months. This current fellowship was supposed to last throughout the whole fall semester. The McCue family had arrived at Graving Lighthouse on Isle Philippeaux at the beginning of September and were supposed to leave on December 20th—just four days away—before the ferry stopped running for winter and before their dad would get home for Christmas.

Mom set her teacup on its tiny saucer and then placed her hands in her lap. Lee sat much the same way, her back straight, as if she could sit still and proper for as long as needed. Glennon itched inside, all of his rigid muscles begging to be let loose and wiggle every which way. He felt ready to burst. Everyone waited, until at last, Uncle Job heaved a gusty sigh and tucked into the food spread across the table.

Glennon missed his dad. He always filled the dinner table

with chatter. Without the distraction, all Glennon heard was the howl of wolves outside the house. *It's not wolves.* He pierced a bean with his fork. *It's the wind.*

But still, the high-pitched, yearning wail that slid through the cracks in the window frames set the hairs on the back of Glennon's neck upright.

GA-ROOOO! The massive foghorn in the lighthouse not two hundred feet from them blew. The sound ripped through the air, and Glennon clapped his hands over his ears.

Lee jumped. All of her proper posture slid straight out of her, her frame turning into crinkled paper, elbows folding in and back hunching over and mouth snapping closed to suck air through her nose. Lee collapsing in on herself happened nearly too fast for Glennon to track; a blur at the edge of his vision revealed her tucking her skinny body beneath the table.

Mom's china rattled with the force of Lee's disappearance. She placed one long-fingered hand atop the pieces to stop their shivering while Glennon looked beneath the table for Lee. She was already gone, though, vanished from the dining room as if she hadn't been there to begin with.

The foghorn sounded again. *GA-ROOOO!* When Lake Superior covered the isle with mist, lighthouse keepers used the horn so sailors could identify Isle Philippeaux's location and avoid running into the island.

Uncle Job's massive hand appeared before Glennon. Resting in the center were two pairs of bright purple disposable earplugs. Glennon shoved two into his ears, and the ugly sounds outside dampened. Uncle Job shook his hand, making the remaining earplugs dance in his palm, and glanced in the direction Lee disappeared. At home, no one was supposed to check on Lee when she gave into her panicked flights; she was supposed to figure out how to calm down on her own. This was Uncle Job's house, though, *not* his dad's house, and an entirely different set of rules existed here. Muscles tense, he reminded himself that no one would yell at him for helping Lee, snatched up the two other earplugs, and left the table to search for Lee in the coat closet beneath the stairs.

The closet door stood open a crack. Far in the back beneath the jackets and behind the shoes, Lee huddled with her arms wrapped around her knees. Back home, she always hid in the small nook between her bed and wall, a blanket over her head. Here, though, she didn't have a small nook, she had a closet.

This version of Lee was so different from the one that normally existed. She seemed years younger than Glennon, instead of fourteen—one year older him. Normally, she reminded Glennon of their dad: she could argue Glennon in circles until his mind tripped over itself, and she was sure of herself in a way Glennon didn't know how to be. But this part of her—the quiet, anxious part that folded in on itself—made the other part not exist, at least for a little while.

"I'm going to touch your ears and put in the plugs to help quiet the sound of the horn," Glennon said, giving her warning before he put the plugs into her ears.

After, he pulled his raincoat off its hanger and slid it over his shoulders before closing the door. He needed to get out of the house.

Glennon returned to the dining table, noticing that Uncle Job had disappeared. Mom sat drinking tea as if everyone hadn't left. The delicate wrist of the hand holding the cup bent at a slight angle, looking like the crooked twig of a tree.

"How's Leeunah?" she asked, her words dampened by the plugs in Glennon's ears.

"Lee's Lee," Glennon said, as if that explained his sister.

His mother nodded, understanding, just as the foghorn let loose another belch.

Glennon jumped.

Mom didn't so much as flinch. "Be grateful for this roof over your head, Glennon." She held her teacup outward, as if she were clinking the glass in celebration with an invisible guest who sat beside her.

"I'm grateful," Glennon said, though being grateful

seemed an entirely different thing than being happy, and what he wanted was to be happy. "I'm going out."

"Don't talk to strangers, but if you do, make sure you mention your uncle's name, so people know you belong on the island and—"

"That I'm not a stranger myself. I know, Mom." It was the same warning she gave every time he or Lee went out.

Glennon backed away from the dining room, uneasy with the lonely picture his family made: Mom sitting alone at the table and Lee crying alone in the closet. He didn't understand how to help either of them, and it made him hurt in a way he didn't know how to fix.

He wrenched open the front door and dove outside. The wind grabbed him up, plucking at the edges of his coat and wrapping around his ankles. Behind him, fog butted up against the tall cliffs of the peninsula on which Graving Lighthouse had stood, though it didn't yet completely cover the lighthouse keepers' homes. Three houses stood in a row beside Graving. One for the First Keeper, and one each for the Second and Third Keepers, the last of which was Uncle Job's. Surrounding all three was a pine and birch forest, filled in with twiggy shrubs and fallen leaves and barren trees ready to sleep for winter.

Stopping at a small shed, he took out his bike. Back home in the city he'd had streetlights to see by when he went out with his friends in the evening. There was hardly any electricity wired on Isle Philippeaux, though, and certainly not any in the woods between Graving Lighthouse and the only town on the island, and that was a good thirty miles away. It was as if the entire island were stuck in 1909 instead of 1989.

He hopped on his bike and flicked on the flashlight he'd taped to the front handles. Gravel bumped and rattled the wheels of the bike, but he pushed at the pedals and headed away from both Lake Superior and the lighthouse. Once in the woods, he was mostly protected from the wind that raged over Superior. The quiet of the forest pressed tight around him. Frigid air burned his lungs and all of a sudden, the decision to bike away from the warmth of the Third Keeper's house seemed like a terrible one.

Something always felt wrong about Isle Philippeaux when he left Graving's protection, and because of it, he stopped peddling quite so hard. He coasted, taking a moment to scan the forest. Treetops leaned over him, their skeletal fingers stretching toward his hair. A breeze slithered against his exposed cheeks and neck. Vapor crept over the sky, seeping off Lake Superior to cover the isle. And inside that sky, with the fog and the skeleton hands made of tree limbs, a face started to appear.

Nope, Glennon thought to himself. There was no part of him interested in dealing with faces in the mist. Skidding to a stop, he wheeled his bike around and started to pedal once again, furiously hurrying back toward Graving and the windstorm. The gravel beneath his bike felt slippery and strange, as if he rode over patches of ice.

At the edge of his vision, a rat emerged from the woods and scurried across the road, heading straight toward him. He wrenched on the handles of his bike to try and keep from running it over—*yuck*—and it darted right between his bike wheels.

Glennon's bike skidded over the pebbles in the road. He straightened the wobbling bike, and there, in the middle of the road five feet in front of him, huddled a boy. Mist sizzled off his shoulders, and his eyes reflected the beam from Glennon's flashlight, an intense green, the same sickly color the sky had once turned right before a tornado blew through his city.

Panic shot up Glennon's spine. He twisted his bike sideways and flew straight through the place the boy had been. Freezing cold washed over him, as if he'd plunged straight into the depths of Superior. A sharp pain snagged the middle of his chest.

He landed hard on the road with the bike flopping onto his leg. Gravel bit into his skin and shredded his pants. He stopped moving and lay still, panting in the shadows of the woods and listening to the *thump-thump* of his heartbeat in his ears, magnified by the purple plugs. The feeling of freezing cold faded until only a small, twisting throb echoed right in the middle of his sternum, only a tendril of the pain he'd felt a moment before.

He rubbed at his chest, and even though he hadn't felt the impact of colliding with the boy, he said aloud, "Did I kill you?" He blinked into the dwindling evening light. No one but him lay in the road...except—

"You stupid cat!" he shouted.

Seamus, their family cat, sat on a large flat rock beside the road. He was massive, with long gray fur that Lee liked to brush. He held one of his white-socked paws in the air and licked it until it shone. Staring at Glennon, his green eyes glowed in the night.

Glennon folded up his legs and rested his forehead on his knees. He sucked air into his lungs to try and settle the adrenaline racing through him.

Be rational, his dad always said when Glennon was scared. *Be rational,* Glennon told himself. There hadn't been a boy in the road, after all. He'd only seen his *cat.*

Feeling bruised all over his body, he forced himself to stand, then picked his bike off the road and hobbled toward the Third Keeper's House. Seamus lead the way.

After a few steps, he stopped walking, sure that something followed them, but no—when he glanced over his shoulder, the road was empty except for the rat he'd almost squashed. It sat on the rock Seamus had vacated.

Glennon shuffled faster, heading back to Graving Lighthouse, filled with the eerie sense that something trailed close behind.

2

As soon as Glennon limped into the safety of Uncle Job's house, his heart rate slowed. Now that he was back, he felt ridiculous. His dad always told him that at thirteen, he shouldn't get scared so easily.

Seamus snuck inside the house behind Glennon, his ears flattened against his head and fur twisted in odd whirlies from the wind. Glennon had tried to carry the cat across the yard where the wind was the fiercest, but Seamus had hissed as soon as he reached out—Seamus had never exactly *liked* Glennon, but he'd never hissed before.

Before he could close the door, wind shrieked through the opening, making him cringe. He shoved against it and pushed hard to latch the bolt.

"Something's wrong with this place. You feel it too, don't you?" Lee said from behind him. Turning, he found the closet door open a sliver. One of Lee's eyes blinked in the space. Tears paved bright streaks down her pale skin and her one visible eye was red-rimmed and glossy. Glennon was always surprised at how she came out of her fear-jags as quickly as she went into them.

He took out his earplugs to hear her better but refused to tell Lee that she was right, that something did feel strange about Isle Philippeaux. It wouldn't sound rational if he did.

"It's probably banshees," Lee said, pointing to the door and the screaming wind outside. Seamus butted his head up against the crack in the closet door. She let Seamus in, and the cat faded into the darkness of the closet.

"It's *not* banshees," he said, even though he didn't know what banshees were. Leave it to Lee to explain away any sort of *wrongness* on the isle with monsters. Glennon had never been all that smart—unfortunately, he hadn't inherited those particular genes from his dad—but at least he didn't have Lee's wild imagination. "First you think wind sprites are outside, then you think there are banshees. Make up your mind."

"Why can't both exist?"

"Because neither do." Glennon sat hard on the steps, exhausted and hurting from the bike crash. Sitting like this, he could no longer see her. "How do you know about all these creatures anyway?"

"I watch movies."

"I watch movies too, and I've never heard of banshees."

"You watch movies like *Indiana Jones*. I watch movies about things that are actually useful."

"What, like movies about monsters?"

"Yes," said Lee, then shut the door with a thwack. After a pause, though, she said through the door, "By the way, you have a giant hole in your pants, and you look *terrible*."

Glennon glanced to find she was right; a finger-length tear was ripped in the seam of his left pant leg right beside the ankle. He *felt* terrible and that terribleness settled deep in his chest. He rubbed at his aching sternum and tried to understand if the terrible feeling inside him was due to the crash or if it was something else. He felt almost as if something awful was about to happen… or already had happened, and he just didn't know what it was.

Ga-roooo, went the foghorn outside. It had almost faded into background noise, by now.

Digging in his left pocket, he pulled out a folded-up postcard from his dad. The curls and flourishes of his dad's handwriting sometimes made it difficult to read. It reminded Glennon of the waves of Lake Superior, folding over itself on the top and hiding darkness beneath.

Brussels has a wonderful history museum! was the single sentence his father had written. The front of the postcard showed an image of the university in Belgium where he was teaching for the semester.

It's a wretched spit of water, Glennon dad's had said when he'd learned Mom was relocating the three of them to Lake Superior for the fall.

Lake Superior likes to sink ships, Lee had said.

Glennon's dad had tried finding Isle Philippeaux on the atlas at home, but the map didn't include the island; it was too small. He'd shut the atlas with a snap and said to Lee, *A lake cannot "like" to sink ships, Lee. A lake merely exists, and it exists within weather patterns. Superior is well known for its horrible storms. It's also well known that sailors are notoriously terrible at predicting weather. Ships sinking is a fact, not a thing a lake likes to do.*

Glennon shook free of the memory and said, "Seamus is such a mean cat. He scared me," as if he were actually talking to his father.

Fear is an animal instinct, his dad would say if he were there, just like he often said when Glennon woke from night-mares. *We aren't animals, Glen—*

"So we shouldn't act like animals," Glennon said out loud.

The memory of seeing a boy in the road filled his head. He tried to forget his fear and think rationally.

"Glen," he said, throwing his voice low in a pretend-dad voice, even though he hated the nickname. "You have to understand that your brain is wired by thousands of years of evolution to protect you from predators. Tonight, the flashlight on your handlebars threw a large shadow behind Seamus. The shadow looked like a boy, and Seamus's eyes glowed like they often do in the dark. It's a simple explanation. You should have thought of it yourself."

"Talking to yourself, dear?" his mother asked, coming around the stairwell from the direction of the dining room.

Sweat broke out beneath Glennon's arms. "No, not really. I mean...Seamus was here. I was talking to him," he said, even though Seamus was with Lee. He wasn't sure if talking to the cat was a good excuse, but he felt sure that admitting he'd been talking to himself would be worse.

Mom started up the stairs passing Glennon on the right. Her steps did not hitch at all as the foghorn said its mournful *ga-roooo*.

"Why did we have to move?" he blurted, feeling extra angry and sharp. They only had a few days left on the island, but he was still annoyed they'd had to come here at all.

His mother turned back to him on the steps. Her head tilted, falling toward one shoulder in slow-motion. "Are you asking why we had to leave home or why we had to move *here*?"

His gaze skittered from Mom's face and the emotionless expression she wore. She never seemed to feel anything, and it confused him, because he seemed to feel *everything*.

"You know I don't like living in that house of ours when your father's gone, Glennon." She took small, soundless strides up the stairs. Even when Glennon listened for the creak of the steps, he couldn't hear them beneath her feet. "We had to move somewhere, and without Grandma around, we had nowhere else to go."

She vanished onto the top landing, and Glennon's breaths grew shallow and tight. Hearing aloud that they'd had nowhere else to go reminded him of the fact that he never understood why she refused to stay at their house alone.

Lee appeared in front of him without any warning, Seamus tucked beneath one arm. How did the girls in his family always walk so quietly? "You better not have made Mom cry," she said. The cat hissed at Glennon.

"I didn't!" Glennon recoiled. He would *never* make their mom cry. "Besides...Mom *doesn't* cry."

Lee's cheeks flooded with angry blushes. "Just because you've never seen Mom cry doesn't mean she doesn't cry." With that, she strode up the steps too.

Glennon shoved up from the stairs, feeling as if he'd been punched three times in his chest, once by the bike accident, once by his mom, and once by his sister. He shuffled through the dining room on legs that felt like they were made of one giant bruise. Entering the kitchen, he stole a slice of bread from the bread box and cut a wedge of cheese from the refrigerator. He ate while watching the fog on the other side of the kitchen window.

Ga-roooo—KA-BOOM! The blare of the foghorn was sliced in half by a deep rumble, as if part of the cliff had sluiced off and thumped into the lake below. Glennon froze, his hand halfway to his mouth, a pinch of bread and cheese caught between thumb and forefinger. He waited for another crash to come or for a reverberation to tremble through his feet. Surely if the cliff were falling apart, he'd feel it…

His gaze caught on the mist outside. A glow appeared on the right side of the window and traveled across to the left. Glennon followed it, scurrying to the door when the glimmer disappeared out of view of the window set into the door. Cupping his face, he pressed against the glass and spied the First Keeper, Orwell, bundled against the winds, his head ducked down with his flashlight clutched in one hand. He raced toward the lighthouse.

Glennon assumed his uncle had already left for the lighthouse; he'd disappeared soon after the foghorn had started *ga-rooooing*, which must have been started by the Second Keeper, who'd been on shift. That meant that all *three* keepers were at the lighthouse now. Glennon couldn't imagine what sort of emergency required all three keepers' presence but it must have had something to do with the *KA-BOOM* that had quaked the air just a moment before.

Fingers moving quickly, Glennon buttoned his slicker tight

around his chest, pulled up the hood, and opened the door to head after the First Keeper. Wind chucked it wide, and he had to put his weight against it to pull it closed. Despite the wind, fog collected around the lighthouse, obscuring the bright beam at the top. Even though he couldn't see it, he knew its light would be pulsing its steady *on-off, on-off, on-on-off* rhythm.

GA-ROOOO! He shoved his earplugs back in to dampen the noise.

The lighthouse was painted white on the top and bottom, with the middle painted a deep midnight blue that made it blend into the night. Once he reached it, he pressed his face against the brick, trying to find a moment of calm before he forced his way around it. He took a deep breath, then plunged toward the side of the lighthouse that faced Lake Superior and its churning, angry waters.

Glennon rounded the lighthouse, and there, through the fog, appeared Uncle Job's head and shoulders, his back obscured by the thick mist. Glennon toed his way forward to his uncle's side, noticing that First Keeper Orwell and Second Keeper Ortez also stood beside him.

Wind clawed at Glennon's hood, but he tightened his grip, holding it beneath his chin, even as tiny fingernails of air slipped beneath the slicker, scratching down his back. Uncle Job held out one arm to Glennon and let him use his large body as a shield.

Glennon peered up at Uncle Job, at the twisting of his dark beard in the wind. Fog billowed around him, and for a flicker of a moment, with mist curling over his face and shoulders, he looked just like the solid mass of a tree, something dragged beneath frigid water and stripped free of leaves.

Glennon shuddered, unsettled by the strange image. Wind gusted. The haze broke up and left Uncle Job alone, and Glennon saw he pointed down and to the right. There, a thick cloud of vapor covered the whole lake and the waves that crashed far below.

Howling against Glennon's earplugs, wind plowed into them. He gripped Uncle Job's coat to keep from being shoved back, and in a blink of time where the entire world seemed to exhale, the fog cleared away from the base of the cliff. He saw then what the three keepers stared at: a small freighter was wedged against a massive rock just a foot or two from the cliff's face. A crack ran through its main deck, and it swayed with each harsh shove of lake water against its hull.

Glennon's mouth dried and a horrible suffocating feeling filled his lungs.

Sailors scurried about the top of the ship, flicking rope and boards and boxes and who knew what else every which way. A shout arose, though the words themselves were ripped apart by the wind. A huge wave swamped the deck, and when the water fell away, Glennon saw one less person than had been there before.

One sailor paused, his back pressed tight to the freighter's railing and looked up. Moonlight silvered the edges of his face, though his eyes stayed shrouded in shadow. He raised one hand to the keepers on the cliff.

The fog rolled back in. Mist pooled against the crevices of the cliff, and the man and his ship disappeared.

3

Uncle Job closed the lighthouse door behind Glennon. It snapped shut, and Glennon's head pounded with the sudden absence of rushing wind. He began to pull out the plugs but shoved them back in when the foghorn sounded its *ga-roooo* again, sounding grief-stricken and shocked, not unlike how Glennon felt. His whole body trembled with fatigue and confusion.

How were they supposed to help the sailors?

"The fog came rolling in thick and fast," said Second Keeper Ortez, a man just about Uncle Job's age—somewhere in his thirties. Long scrapes of faded scars trailed through his dark hair, almost as if a bear had clawed his skin when he was young. "I didn't expect it. I should've started the foghorn sooner. This is my fault."

"It's not." Uncle Job's voice rumbled through Glennon's side. Surprised, Glennon realized he'd pressed back against his uncle, seeking comfort as if he were a little kid. He forced himself to take a step away, even though he didn't like the sudden cold that settled deep into his body.

"It is absolutely not your fault. Ships wreck," said the First Keeper. The smooth, black skin of his face showed no trace of whatever he felt. "The *Anabeth* has traveled on this lake for many years. Her captain knew the risks of sailing during winter."

"What are we going to do?" Glennon blurted. Everyone was standing around like they were waiting for someone else to arrive and help. There wasn't anyone else around though—they were the only people there!

The First Keeper cocked his head to the side and his speckled black-and-white hair caught the dim light inside the lighthouse. "We are going to do nothing. There's no way to climb down the cliff to reach to them, and it isn't safe for anyone to sail to them. There's nothing we can do short of attempting to help and dying in the process."

"But—"

"Are you interested in dying?"

Glennon's gaze snapped to his. "No!"

The First Keeper snorted and turned from the group, heading up the steps of the lighthouse toward the light at the very top.

"That's it?" Glennon asked Uncle Job. "That's all you're going to do? Those sailors will die."

"Orwell has been First Keeper here for a very long time, Glennon. He's witnessed many wrecks and many deaths. He's right." Uncle Job turned to him, large eyes drooping at the corners. "Until technology improves with weather prediction and gadgets are created that will help boats see their surroundings better, it'll be a risk for them to travel, especially this late in storm season. Sometimes this isle can be an unhappy place to live. We've phoned in the wreck. That's the best we can do until the weather subsides and someone can get down the cliff to help."

Their *best* was doing nothing at all! Glennon said, "What are we supposed to do now?"

"We?" said the Second Keeper, who stood at the bottom of the stairs. "*We* don't do anything. *You* go to bed, where you should be anyway."

Glennon turned to Uncle Job, but his uncle only nodded and shoed Glennon toward the back entrance of the lighthouse, the one that didn't lead out onto the cliff. At the door, he hesitated, but when he turned back, it was to see his uncle climbing the steps after the First and Second Keepers.

Glennon watched them go, the soles of their boots showing through the metal slats, furious that they were giving up. They weren't even trying to help the sailors! But as he watched, the creeping feeling that something was wrong, was *missing*, filled his chest. He held still and watched, listening to the wind wailing against Graving and the surf pummeling the cliffside, knowing that somewhere inside all that noise were the screams of the sailors below. At last he identified the wrongness: he hadn't heard a single clomp of the keepers' footfalls against the iron stairwell. The sound of the storm outside must have covered the sound of their steps. That had to be it.

He escaped outside and at once, his eardrums were hit by the wind. It ripped at his slicker, though he didn't quite notice its invisible hands like he had earlier. He was too distracted. Back at the house, his fingers, slick with mist, slid against the door handle, and it took three tries to twist the knob. The door shot open, bashing into the wall. He forced it closed, then pressed his back to the frame while he took in a long, deep breath and wrestled with the knowledge of the shipwreck and the dying men.

His lungs tightened as an old feeling came to him, one he knew belonged to the memories locked inside his head. The ones he did his best never to look at straight. It sat deep in his body, and though he tried to force it out, it worsened. He found the right word for the feeling: *helplessness*. Thinking of the shipwreck made him feel helpless.

BANG! Something smashed into the back of the door.

Glennon leapt out of his skin. He spun, fists pressed against his pounding heart. When he peered through the window, nothing stood on the other side. *Be rational,* he thought. *Don't be scared.* The bang had probably been some stray object shoved against the door by the wind—

A boy's face appeared in the door's window, white and water-lined, with eyes too bright and nearly absent of color. A scream strangled deep inside Glennon's throat.

"You have to help! I saw you walking just now. I don't know where anyone else is, and we need help!" The boy worked his mouth which had turned blue from the cold. "The others are climbing up the rope!" He turned and ran down the path toward the cliffside, leaving Glennon behind with wind whistling beneath the door.

Adrenaline raced through Glennon's body. He didn't know what help the boy needed, but he was determined to try. Maybe if he helped, the entire isle wouldn't feel so rotten. Maybe it would fix the *wrongness* of this place.

Glennon yanked open the door and followed. A dark smidgen of the boy's shadow flitted through the mist—the back of his head, his shoulders, his feet as he ran. Glennon surged into the fog, trying to keep his balance against the wet stone walkway. The top of Graving peeked through the thick mists. Several large rocks bordered the base of the lighthouse, reinforcing the white-painted brick. Catching sight of one at the periphery of his vision, he stumbled, confused, because if the rock was *there*, then the cliff had to be—

He skidded, trying to stop, but he was moving too fast and he tripped over a crack in a stone. He fell and his chest smacked into the ground, his chin following suit. Pain shot through his body for the second time that evening.

He lifted one hand and went to push it into the ground to lever himself up…and his arm dropped down into thin air.

Glennon shouted and looked up; white mist and empty air curled before his nose. *The cliff.* He would have plummeted straight over the side had he not tripped. He pressed his forehead into the dirt, vomit rising in his throat, and found that there, to his left, crouched the boy.

"Wouldn't want you to fall over!" the blue-lipped boy shouted, his words pulled thin by Lee's wind sprites.

Glennon heaved a terrified breath, the air getting sucked straight out of his lungs by the harsh gusts at the cliffside. A thick rope lay on the ground between him and the boy, its prickly fibers soaked by water. The end of it was tied to one of the metal hooks bolted into the rock at the edge of the cliff. Glennon peered over, except the fog was too thick, and he couldn't see anything past a foot or two down.

But then, the mist swirled, shucked around by a form pushing up through the fog, almost like one of Lee's zombie movies, some creature shoving its dead arm through dirt and grass.

A large, brown hand gripped the rope and a man's body came up the edge of the cliff. The boy leaned out over the side and took hold of the man's belt loops, tugging hard. Glennon gripped the back of the man's shirt. All three of them grunted as they dragged him over the ledge and onto solid ground.

"Where am I?" The sailor trembled as he sat. On his forehead, a goose egg raised up and dripped blood down his temple.

"This is Isle Philippeaux," Glennon shouted over the wind.

The sailor's eyes grew wide. "No. *No. No, no, no.*" The sailor tried to stand. He stumbled, tripping over his own feet.

Glennon reached out a hand in comfort, but the sailor jerked away, terror wrinkling his forehead and pinching his cheeks.

"Another is coming up!" cried the boy. He hung his head over the edge of the cliff, peering down the length of the rope.

"I-Isle *Philippeaux*?" The sailor dropped to his knees and began to crawl away, as if he were trying to escape. "*Phan… Is…nd.*"

"Oye! Help, would you?" said the boy, and Glennon forced himself to turn away from the injured sailor.

A white, bloodless arm flung up from beyond the lip of the cliff and thwacked onto the rope. Water slicked over the skin, and for a moment, the arm looked translucent and filmy, almost like frozen ice cubes that had begun to melt. A second man dragged himself up the cable, the tendons standing out on the back of his forearm. He clawed his way onto the cliff with the boy and Glennon helping.

When safe on the ground, the man lay still, with eyelids closed and a fierce grin stretching across his face.

"Are you alright?" Glennon shouted, hoping this sailor wouldn't be as confused as the first.

"Made it, didn't I?" the man said. The man opened his eyes then, revealing a blue so light they resembled one of Glennon's shirts that had been nearly washed free of dye. They looked dead, drained...*lifeless*.

Glennon leaned back and away, his body feeling terrified though he didn't understand why. This wasn't one of Lee's scary stories, though; there was no reason to be scared.

Be rational.

He returned the man's smile and did his best to ignore the ribbons of fear that tied knots inside his chest.

4

The sailor with the nearly translucent arm drank coffee in Uncle
Job's kitchen. Every time he blinked, his eyes reflected the light
above. *Blink*, they were the white of headlights. *Blink*, they were
the silver of a mirror in the dark. *Blink*, they were the clear pane
of a window, shone through with a candle.

Everyone had gathered in Uncle Job's house—the three
keepers, the three sailors, and the three McCues. The storm
still raged outside, and so they could do nothing for the men
who hadn't been able to climb up the rope. All they could do
was wait for the storm to subside and discover if anyone had
survived on the ship.

Wrongness settled inside Glennon again, rooting deep, while
he watched the trick of the man's eyes. The feeling matched the
one the isle gave him anytime he ventured too far from Graving
Lighthouse, and he wanted to dig it out of his lungs, wanted
a spoon or a shovel or the claws of a badger to set it loose.
Graving was the only place on Isle Philippeaux that he felt safe,

but now, his safe place had been invaded by a man whose eyes made him think of the nightmares he did his best to ignore. He didn't feel safe at all.

Glennon focused on breathing deep and slow, hearing his dad tell him that *your lungs work just fine; quit breathing so raspy* as he stood with his back pressed against the kitchen wall.

Drippy clothes from the three shipwrecked sailors draped on hooks along the wall, and dry clothes borrowed from Uncle Job now hung over Everett and Gibraltar's shoulders—the two adult sailors—all loose and baggy. The boy, Kit Pike, had borrowed a sweatshirt and pair of jeans from Glennon.

"They're creepy, and they're drinking Mom's coffee," Lee whispered in Glennon's ear, startling him. She stood close beside him, crowding his right side. He'd long since taken out his earplugs, wanting to hear the conversation better. The fog had begun dissipating, and as soon as it disappeared entirely, the Second Keeper would turn off the foghorn.

"They're not creepy, Lee. Don't call them that," he said out of habit, grateful she hadn't called them ghouls or something. He kept watch of Everett's face, but the man's eyes had stopped shifting. They were eyes, just normal human eyes, the color of murky water.

Mom poured Everett more coffee, and briefly, their hands touched. She winced and pulled back, clasping her fingertips into her palm and her palm to her stomach, almost as if she'd been burned

Old feelings rose in Glennon, his bones wanting to climb straight out of his skin. *Protect mom, keep her safe, help her!* screamed the part of him that always spoke up when he saw his mom flinch. It had always been Glennon's job to keep Mom safe; his dad had said so the first time he'd gone away on a work trip. *Keep mom safe.* Except what was Glennon supposed to keep Mom safe from, right now? She'd probably just touched the hot pot of coffee and burned herself. He shoved at the feeling, trying to bury it in his stomach, though it left him exhausted and itchy inside.

Everett turned toward Glennon then and smiled. It crooked at the edges, looking as if it'd been chiseled from ice and wasn't, in fact, a smooth smile worn on a face.

"Be a good boy and stoke up the fire," Everett said.

Hesitating, Glennon looked to Uncle Job, dismayed when his uncle nodded at him. He knew Uncle Job wouldn't let anything happen to Mom, but still…Glennon really didn't trust anyone. He didn't know how.

He headed to the living room and poked at the fire with an iron pole. Sparks shot into the chimney. The heat of it rushed over his skin, not quite burrowing deep enough to toast up his bones. They ached from the cold…or was it from the memory of Mom's flinch and Everett's smile? He couldn't quite tell.

"I think he's creepy too," Lee said, her breath tickling the back of his neck.

This time when he jumped, a yelp escaped his mouth. Why did his sister have to keep sneaking up on him!

"Something's wrong here." She held Seamus against her chest, both arms wrapped around his belly so that his legs hung limp.

"What's wrong is that there was a shipwreck and people died," he said.

"No. That's not it. Shipwrecks happen here. They've happened here for hundreds of years. That's just a matter of fact. Something else is wrong, like...*ghouls*."

Glennon slapped his forehead.

"Or zombies," Lee muttered.

"Zombies aren't real!" The sudden memory of Everett's pale, sodden arm and colorless, dead eyes flew through Glennon's mind. He hated it.

"They could be."

"You're being stupid."

"I am *not* stupid," she said calmly. She took a breath, and in that space, wind whipped outside, unleashing a howl against the wall and sending up the hairs on Glennon's neck.

He cringed into himself, knowing she was right—she wasn't the one between them who was stupid.

"Science is quite clear that zombies are possible. There are zombie ants and zombie spiders, so why can't there be zombie people? I admit it's unlikely that the apocalypse is about to happen or that it's about to start here or that zombies will be the type of monster that destroys us, but zombies *could* be real. You can't argue that."

It wasn't fair that Lee thought so much faster he did. She'd always been able to argue him in circles.

Chairs scraped in the kitchen and feet stomped as the men made their way into the living room. Mom walked behind everyone, carrying a package of Hawaiian rolls that she opened and started handing out. Gibraltar, the sailor with the goose egg lump on his head, tried to walk straight out the front door, but Everett grabbed his arm and forced him to sit on the couch. Fear radiated off Gibraltar, strong enough that Glennon almost felt he could smell it.

Everett passed by Glennon on his way to sit beside Gibraltar. A slight chill floated off his skin, seeming to seep into Glennon's. He sat on the couch before the fireplace, but as he did, he saw Lee standing beside Glennon. Seamus hissed, and Everett recoiled.

He said, "That cat's *huge*! He can't be natural."

Lee squeezed Seamus tighter, holding him like a teddy bear, while anger turned her cheeks pink.

"Pick back up the story." The First Keeper sat down at a

desk that faced the front window and thumped a book on its top, squashing the papers Glennon had left out from his homeschooling work.

The entire living room quickly became crowded. Nine people was more than the living room had been built to hold. Leeunah escaped the crowd. She snuck straight through the living room and up the stairs with Seamus, though no one besides Glennon seemed to notice.

"I'm not sure what else there's to tell about the *Anabeth's* demise." Fury burned through Everett's expression, tightening the waxy skin beneath his eyes. "I've already told you how it happened. Twenty men died in the mess of it."

Glennon swallowed down the burn of vomit. He'd stood a hundred feet above while *twenty men* got sucked into Lake Superior. Who knew if anyone was still alive? Were they still down there, fighting for their lives? He realized that with the storm still raging, they couldn't help the sailors or their ship, but he didn't understand why none of the keepers were standing at the edge of the cliff, keeping watch.

"If you think of more details, please let me know." The First Keeper's pen stilled on the page. Upside down, Glennon saw the scrawl of the number *20*.

"You couldn't have done anything to help," Everett said, his gaze locked on First Keeper.

First Keeper Orwell closed his recording book, his own anger evident.

"It was the captain's decision to sail," Everett said. "Not yours. Nothing could be done to help them."

Why was Everett comforting the First Keeper? Shouldn't it be the other way around, considering that Everett had just lost most of his crewmen?

"I want to leave," murmured Gibraltar. His dark gaze wandered about the room, taking in all the shadowy corners and each of the people hovered inside them. "It isn't safe here."

No one besides Glennon seemed to hear him, or at least, no one acknowledged his words. Glennon felt awful for the man.

Glennon remembered Kit, then. At first glance, he didn't spot him, but then found him sitting on the floor close to the fire with his back pressed against the arm of the couch.

"I would like to find a place to sleep," Everett said.

"Kit can stay here," Glennon offered, wanting to help.

"No," Uncle Job said, and First Keeper Orwell nodded. Glennon didn't understand. What was wrong with the idea?

"Oh no, that's an excellent idea. Kit could sleep right on this couch beside the fire," Everett said. When he talked, everything he said sounded like a threat, and suddenly, Glennon wished he could take back the offer. "Kit will stay here and Gibraltar will come with me to stay elsewhere. I'll pick Kit up in the morning.

Hopefully the storm will be finished by then, and we can check on the *Anabeth*."

"Me?" asked the sailor with the lump on his head.

"Yes, you," said Everett.

"But I don't know you. I don't want to stay with you," said Gibraltar.

"*Shhh.*" Everett patted his knee. "You're confused."

"I don't know you," whispered Gibraltar. His face was still frozen with terror, the same expression that had come over him when Glennon had said he'd landed on Isle Philippeaux.

"He could stay here, with Kit," First Keeper Orwell said. His skin seemed to contract, all the muscles in his face tensing.

Quiet anger seemed to fill in all the gaps of the drafty room, though Glennon didn't understand why. Why was everyone so concerned with where people would sleep? Shouldn't everyone be more worried about the people who'd died? Glennon pressed his back into his chair, trying to push himself into the cushions and be invisible in the same way his mom and sister could make themselves invisible.

"He's not well. He needs to stay with someone he knows." Everett's gaze slid toward Glennon, toward Glennon's mom. "There are already too many people crowding this house."

"I'm not sure I agree," the First Keeper said, his voice dropping low.

Why did everyone seem mad at one another? It was as if there were two conversations happening in the room. One Glennon heard with his ears, and one he wasn't privy to—one that only Everett and the keepers understood.

The moment tightened. Glennon's muscles turned rigid, and he pushed harder against the chair, wincing, sure in his gut that something bad was about to happen. The strain infected his mind, and just as it'd happened earlier when Everett appeared on the cliff, everything seemed to turn sideways: Everett's skin paled further, a gleaming luster coating his face and dripping into his eyes; Kit looked nearly too bright to look at, turning harsh around the edges just like the outer rim of the sun; Keeper Orwell froze, whorls of ice curling off the tips of his peppered hair—

Glennon smashed his eyes closed, not wanting to find out what his confused, tired brain would transform Mom or Uncle Job or even Gibraltar into. He rubbed his eyes, knowing he desperately needed sleep.

When he opened his eyes, he found everyone standing and preparing to leave. How had he missed the end of the argument? What had happened?

At the door, Everett touched his brow and nodded at Mom who held out a small baggie of cookies to the man. "Do you live on the isle?" he asked, as if this were a normal moment when two people were first meeting, instead of a conversation happening right after a massive shipwreck.

"I'm visiting Job, my brother." Mom handed the bag of cookies to Gibraltar, who hovered beside Everett, restless and fidgety.

"They're here until the twentieth," Uncle Job interrupted.

"They leave before The Waning celebration?" Everett asked, his brows knitting together.

"Yes," Uncle Job said.

Glennon pulled the phrase *The Waning* out of his memory, shuddering against the sticky feeling of the words. It pulled free, strands stringing back into his mind, as if it were made of gum or hot glue. No one had ever answered him straight about what The Waning was. As far as he could tell, it was a solstice celebration on December 21, the longest night of the year. But that's not what the celebration name felt like to him—it *felt* like endings, of the way happiness during a birthday seeped away at night, of the way the sugar-sweet scent of pumpkin pie disappeared the day after it was eaten, of the way he couldn't quite remember the press of his grandma's hugs anymore.

It didn't matter, though, because The Waning would happen after the McCues left. They'd be long gone by then. *Four more days.*

"*Ahh* well, I've visited this isle many times before and have been present during The Waning. It's a wonderful celebration. I think you would enjoy it," Everett said, looking at Uncle Job but speaking to Mom.

Four more days, Glennon thought desperately. He was sure, absolutely sure that no part of him would enjoy The Waning.

Everett reached past Gibraltar and opened the door, sliding into the windy night and following Second Keeper Ortez to his house. First Keeper Orwell muttered something to Uncle Job that Glennon couldn't quite catch, and then, between one blink of a moment and the next, only Kit was left in the living room, curled up on the couch beneath a blanket.

Alone, Glennon stood with fog oozing into his brain, as it often did after adrenaline and fear washed through his body. He hated this part, when he got too tired to think straight. He headed toward his room but caught sight of a small moleskin notebook on the table. *Isle Philippeaux—Atlas* read the cover. It must have fallen out of the First Keeper's ledger.

Picking it up, Glennon tucked it beneath his arm and promised himself he'd return it in the morning.

At the top of the stairs, a small hallway led to three rooms—Glennon and Lee's, Mom's, and Uncle Job's. Glennon went left, knowing he'd likely find Lee sound asleep with Seamus at her side, protecting her from her own nightmares.

"What a terrible evening," Mom said from the doorway of her room, startling him.

He pressed one hand into the wall, frustrated over how many scare jumps he'd had that night. It wasn't fair that everyone but him could move like a ghost.

She stood, quiet and still in her doorway. *Protect Mom,* all of his instincts still sang. But what was he supposed to protect her from?

5

In the middle of the night, Glennon found himself standing in his mother's bedroom, his socked feet warm against the cold wooden floor. Goose bumps prickled his bare arms. He only wore a thin T-shirt, which wasn't much good against the chill that swept through the Third Keeper's house. He didn't remember how he'd gotten here. Had he sleepwalked? He did that sometimes.

Tense and confused, he peered at his mother. The small, twin-size bed held her slight frame, her weight hardly making a mound beneath the purple and yellow patterned quilt.

Glennon tried to walk back to his bedroom, but the air thickened about him as if he moved through thick soup. His heart beat faster inside his chest, its staccato rhythm tapping against his ribs. His eyes rotated inside his skull and locked on the moonlight that streamed through the open window. It streaked along the floor, highlighting the little lamp beside his mother's bed, the book that had slid off a shelf and landed flat on the floor with its cover wide open...and the extended limbs of a monster.

Sweat pooled beneath Glennon's arms and against his hands and turned his feet wet and slimy inside his socks. The creature stepped forward and out from the darkness came... *Everett*. Lifting one hand to his mouth, the sailor held up a finger, saying an unheard *shhh* to Glennon. With his opposite hand, he pulled from his pocket a thin, wispy strand of thread, at the end of which dangled a fishing hook.

With silent motions and with Glennon watching and unable to move, Everett crossed the room to Glennon's mom. He pierced the hook into her chest and fastened it around her breastbone. He continued to hold the end of the string, as if Glennon's mom were a fish snared at the end of a line.

"What did you do?" Glennon said, furious and barely able to move his mouth.

I haven't done anything. Everett waved a hand, smoke trailing off the tips of his fingers. In the darkness, his eyes glittered like they were made of ice. *Nothing at all, Glen.*

"I hate that name," Glennon snarled.

I like it though. Everett ran one hand over the thin rope knotted into Mom's chest. *You're imagining things. You're dreaming.*

Glennon felt Everett's fingernails as if he scratched them

across the back of Glennon's hand instead of over the rope. Glennon squeezed his hand shut and opened it again, trying to rid his skin of the feeling of Everett's sickening touch. When he looked up, he blinked, confused. He sat in the middle of the stairwell, facing the front door. The back of his hand scraped against one of the banisters next to him.

"Oh," Glennon said. The cobwebby fog of sleep washed from his mind. His thoughts came into focus. He'd been sleep-walking after all. He'd been sleeping and dreaming and…what had he been dreaming about?

He climbed to his feet and went to his mother's bedroom. She slept, hardly moving at all, though the tips of her hair fluttered in the breeze—her window stood open, and on the frame sat a green-eyed rat. It scampered away as soon as Glennon appeared, its tiny nails scraping at the wood.

Glennon crossed the room and closed the window, latching it tight. Through its clear pane, he saw Lake Superior was quiet and still and that the outer rim of the sun was beginning to show over her waters. He didn't dare peer down to find if the *Anabeth* was visible.

He couldn't stand seeing anything else creepy that night.

The first thought Glennon had upon waking was *three days*, and the second was *I think I broke something*. His chest ached right in the middle of his breastbone. It was the place that had hurt furiously after the bike accident. He rubbed at the spot and let his mind swing back to his first thought of *three days*. He only needed to survive three more days on the island, and then he'd be free. They'd head home.

Ignoring his bruised chest, he climbed from beneath his covers, grabbed his notebook, and sat in the window seat on the other side of Lee's empty bed. He wrote:

> Last night, Lake Superior raged and tried to swallow down a ship. The ship survived by crashing on a giant boulder that poked out of the lake, but the men aboard didn't manage to survive as well.

He cocked his head, looking at the sentences from a different angle, trying to see if they sounded the same on paper as they did in his head. This was the problem with writing: words made certain shapes when he thought them that they didn't make when he read them aloud.

The full story of the men's ascent up the cliff flowed into the notebook. When he finished, he creased the pages as close to the binding as he could, tore them out, then set them inside a shoe box he kept under his bed.

Inside his notebook, he wrote again:

Last night, a ship crashed before the cliff below Graving Lighthouse. The ship ran aground, smashing into a boulder. Twenty men were lost. Three survived by climbing the cliff itself.

This account was factual and specific, and no part of it read like Glennon had made it up. That would make his dad happy. He placed both copies of the tale back beneath his bed and left his room.

In the hallway, he found Leeunah standing at the top of the stairs. She wore her backpack on the front of her chest, and inside it, Seamus sat with his head peeking out, gray fur fluffing around his face. The cat stared unblinking at Glennon.

Glennon stared right back. He was still mad at Seamus for making him fall off his bike.

Lee said, "What's wrong with you?"

Glennon stopped glaring and then stopped rubbing at the aching spot on his chest. He said, "How's Mom today?"

"I think she's alright." Lee peered at him oddly, and he realized he'd asked the question in the same way they usually checked in with each other after their parents argued. *How's*

Mom? one of them would ask, and the other would say, *I think she's alright,* even if they both knew she wasn't.

He still had the terrible sense that something was wrong with Mom. He tried to shove away the feelings though. He knew better than to trust his emotions. His dad always said that his feelings were usually wrong; they made him too sensitive, and they were probably why he had so many nightmares.

"I'm going to go see the *Anabeth.* Do you want to come?" Lee asked.

Glennon followed her outside, noticing that Kit wasn't anywhere downstairs. The thermometer nailed to the front door read a sweltering fifty degrees—sweltering for a Minnesota winter, at least—and was so different from the biting cold of the night before.

In front of Graving, the sharp line of the cliff looked different than it had during the storm, more crisp at the edges, more angled. Almost as if someone had come along and changed the shape of it, chiseling at the sides until it became a zigzag and not a curve.

You're probably remembering it wrong. You know you have a terrible memory, Glennon told himself. It was true enough. He always felt like he had a brain made of Swiss cheese, with information falling straight through the holes.

"I almost died here last night," Glennon said. "Almost tripped right over the edge."

"Why, 'cause you weren't watching your feet?" Lee said.

"I was watching my feet. I was just moving too fast." Glennon held out his arms at ninety-degree angles, like he was the Flash and about to take off and run away.

Lee laughed. Glennon always liked it when he could make his sister happy. He dropped his arms and tiptoed forward a bit. He stayed well away from the edge, peering over the massive, unending lake from the safety of the landing.

To Glennon, Lake Superior felt like *waiting*. He held himself tight, ready for her to unleash sudden fury like she had the night before. *Lake Superior likes to sink ships*, Lee had said.

"She was so angry," Glennon said to Leeunah.

"Who?" Lee asked. "Mom wasn't angry."

"Lake Superior. She was…" He waved his arms at the lake below. "She was furious."

"She wasn't angry," Lee said. "Women aren't allowed to be angry. If you're going to describe Lake Superior as some angry mythical lake-creature, you'll need to make it a *him*."

"Women can too be angry!"

"Mom's not allowed to be angry."

Glennon wrinkled his nose. "You get angry with me."

"Not really."

It was true—he and Lee might get into arguments, but

they never raged at each other, which was the emotion he'd felt pouring from Superior the night before.

"The kind of anger you're talking about is the kind of anger that swallows up everything else. I've only ever seen Da—"

"This conversation sucks," Glennon interrupted Lee.

She continued, ignoring him. "If you're going to make Superior a woman, you need to say she's monstrous."

"How is the word *monster* better than the word *angry?*"

"I like monsters." Lee grinned, all her teeth showing. Seamus seemed to grin too, his sharp little fangs sticking out from beneath upper lip.

All of a sudden, the rocks beneath Glennon's feet shifted. He locked his knees and held out his arms for balance, experiencing the same sickening feeling as the night before, as if a stiff wind were about to pick him up by the armpits and shove him over the edge of the cliff.

"Are you trying to fly?" Lee asked, glancing at Glennon's arms.

"No. I..." Glennon dropped his arms, noticing that Lee didn't stand braced. "You mean you didn't feel that?"

"Feel what?"

"The rocks jolted. I put my arms out so I wouldn't fall over."

"The rocks didn't jolt." Lee zippered up the backpack a smidge, and Seamus tucked his head inside. "Nothing moved."

Glennon took an uncertain step away from the cliff.

"I'm going down to the lake." Lee headed toward a steep set of stairs that led to the beach below Graving.

Glennon didn't follow. He needed a moment to settle himself before he went to get a closer view of the *Anabeth*.

"Looking at the ship?" asked a voice behind him.

Glennon turned toward Graving, but as he did, his eyes blurred. The image of the white and black lighthouse faded beneath a fuzzy blob, almost as if he'd stared into the sun too long. He rubbed at his eyes, and when he looked up, he saw Kit leaning against the lighthouse, arms folded and hair sticking in every direction. In the morning light, it was the color of brown yarn set in a window for too long, fading to a dim shade of yellow.

"I thought you left," Glennon said, still rubbing at his eyes. "Went to go meet Everett and Gibraltar."

"Not yet." Kit strode up and stood beside Glennon. Having Kit beside him made him feel braver, and he peered down to the lake.

The ship lay on its side now, the hull bent over the boulder, the waves having shoved it against the rock during the storm. Lake Superior's waters were so still and so clear this morning that the entirety of the ship could be seen, even that which lay broken beneath the surface.

Glennon had to turn away, because he realized what also lay beneath that surface were bodies.

"Terrible, in'it." Kit stared longingly down at the ship. Glennon wanted to know what it was he saw when he looked at it. Kit had stood *on* that ship the day before. If Glennon felt bad, Kit must feel so much worse. "I'd hardly been on the ship for any time, you know. Hardly knew anyone onboard."

Glennon asked, "Why were you on the *Anabeth*?"

"It was take your son to work day."

"Your *dad* was on the ship? Is he okay?"

"Yes! I mean, no… Never mind." He rubbed his forehead. When he did, Glennon saw that Kit's right ear was mashed and torn and blackened around the edges. The sight of it sickened something deep in him. Kit needed a doctor. "I don't want to talk about it."

Glennon's words stuck inside him, as they often did when he became confused. The ability to talk evaporated. It was as if his thoughts spun both too fast and too slow, and even though he opened his mouth to speak, nothing came out.

Kit stepped away from the cliff and started walking left along the cliff. He curved, heading around the opposite side of the lighthouse, disappearing, but not before turning and shouting, "I'll see you later, Glennon!"

"Are you going to find Everett?" Glennon asked, but Kit was already gone.

Unsettled and feeling alone, Glennon glanced back to the lake, where a black ship sailed now around the coast of the isle and toward the wreck. The words COAST GUARD were painted on the side, along with the name *Mesquite*. All around the *Mesquite* and the *Anabeth*, Lake Superior's waters sparkled.

He turned to follow after Lee but froze as soon as he turned his back to the lake. The hairs rose along the back of his neck. Something terrible watched him from behind. He turned slowly, but of course, only Superior and her laughing waters stared at him.

You're being irrational, Glennon, he told himself. Superior wasn't about to attack him. She couldn't very well raise tentacles out of the water and drag him down. She wasn't a monster... *Everett* might be a monster, but not the entire lake.

Glennon paused as soon as he heard himself think the word *monster*. He'd seen the movie *The Abyss*; Lee had made him. His dad said monsters weren't real, but the movie had been convincing. In it, strange creatures had lived beneath the water.

Stop, insisted his dad's angry voice inside his head. *You're like Lee if you believe Everett's a monster from the lake.*

Pushing his knuckles against his forehead, he tried to shove thoughts of monsters out of his mind. He wasn't supposed to have Lee's wild imagination. But the harder he tried, the louder his thoughts got. And the louder his thoughts got, the more he felt the press of Lake Superior at his back, as if the lake itself was where Everett had crawled from and not off the bow of a ship.

6

Glennon walked down the wooden stairs that led to the beach.
They dropped down a sloping hill to the left of the keepers'
houses and into the bay between Graving's peninsula and the
rest of the island. The stairs cut through the woods, doubling
back once or twice because of how long and steep the decline
was. Pausing at one of these places, about halfway down to
the lake, he turned around to look back up to where Graving
Lighthouse peeked through the pines.

The lighthouse stood sentinel on the edge of the cliff, the
white top and black middle appearing clear against the light
blue sky. He imagined her sleeping now, her great eye closed
while she recovered from the storm the night before. Staring at
her, he wondered how many shipwrecks she'd witnessed, how
many deaths and funerals she'd presided over, how many times
she'd been the very last thing a sailor saw before they dropped
into the graveyard waters below.

With her guarding his back—even if she was still

asleep—he let gravity pull him down the stairs and closer to the wreck.

The stairs led directly to the edge of the lake and the strange beaches there. Isle Philippeaux didn't have beaches in the sense that Glennon knew beaches, with pebbled sand someone could bury their feet beneath. Instead, there were bumpy expanses of rock that made him think of cooled lava.

Not far from the beach rested the twisted heap of metal that was the *Anabeth*. A broken seam split through the bright red paint of her body. Death and endings and the awful sound of waves crashing into the ship's belly filled his mind, and he turned his gaze to Lee who crouched flat-footed with her arms wrapped around her knees. He stepped over the places where water pooled in the divots of the pockmarked stone and went to her side. Seamus sat next to her, staring away from the lake and at a trio of small gray rats that ate acorns between the upraised roots of an oak tree.

Distant, murmuring voices traveled over the water: the coast guard talking aboard their own ship as they took stock of the *Anabeth*, all broken and warped by the storm.

Lee stared, entranced, whereas Glennon felt repulsed.

"Look," Lee whispered.

Glennon looked up in time to see three men dressed entirely in black scuba gear jump off the side of the coast guard ship. He shuddered, not able to imagine how someone would willingly choose to enclose themselves beneath the frigid water, especially not when they were going down to search for bodies. The absolute only way Glennon would ever find himself inside Lake Superior's waters was if he had no choice in the matter.

Glennon looked away from the ship, not wanting to watch the scuba divers disappear, and down at the water in front of Seamus. A face stared at him from the shallows, eyes lidless and staring. Cheeks and lips bloated. Hair twisting in the lake's current.

Everett.

Glennon stumbled back, right heel catching against a rock. Seamus flicked out his paw and speared the water, distorting the face inside it. A tiny fish darted through the lake, racing away from Seamus, and when Glennon looked back at the water, nothing floated beneath the surface except for the pockmarked rock of the beach. The face was gone.

"It's like watching the scuba divers in *Jaws*," Lee said.

Glennon wiped his sweating palms against his jeans. He ducked his head between his knees to calm his breathing and asked, "When did you see *Jaws*?", trying not to think of the very real possibility of seeing actual dead bodies wash ashore.

"With Cassandra and Lawrence," she said.

Lee had seen all sorts of scary movies. The only scary movies Glennon liked were ones like *Teen Wolf*...and that wasn't actually a scary movie. If their dad would've known about Lee's secret habit of walking into theaters to watch scary movies, he would've been furious. He'd caught her once, had found a ticket stub on the desk in her bedroom.

Glennon remembered his dad's rage, vibrating through the wall that connected his bedroom to Lee's: *Leeunah! Your wild imagination needs no help from Hollywood!*

Glennon had found his sister later, wedged between her bed and the wall, a blanket tucked over her head with Seamus hiding inside the tent with her. He hadn't known what to do, and so he'd slid a granola bar beneath the blanket, the tips of Lee's fingers showing when she took it.

And the thing was…Lee still went to the movies. She went, even though she knew how mad their dad would be if he found out. Glennon wouldn't have dared.

"I wonder if Lake Superior preserves bodies." murmured Lee.

"You shouldn't talk about that," Glennon said back, though his heart wasn't in the comment. By now, he expected his sister's creepiness, though every time she said something odd, he heard his dad in his head, telling her to stop.

It was exhausting.

"I'm going to go." He climbed to his feet and refused to look at the lake again.

The beach curved in a crescent shape along the small inlet. He walked far enough away from Lee that he ended up on the opposite side, and there, he found Townsend, the only other kid he'd ever seen on the island. She lived at a lighthouse opposite the island from Graving. Her dad was a meteorologist who studied the weather patterns of Superior. Townsend didn't have a mom on the isle, as far as Glennon knew, but they did live with a lighthouse keeper who Glennon had only met once before.

Glennon hadn't ever spent time with Townsend before. It wasn't that she was unfriendly, it was more that she'd never sought out his or Lee's company...not that he'd ever sought her out before either.

She sat in a rowboat with the black hood of her raincoat pulled over her brow. Her whole face fell in shadow. One of her hands rested on the top of the old motor attached to the back side of her boat. He'd seen her buzzing around the edge of Isle Philippeaux before and wasn't surprised to see her here now. He *was* surprised, though, to see that Kit stood before her on the very edge of the beach, almost with his feet in the water. Glennon had thought Kit had left to meet up with Everett.

"Hello," Glennon said.

Neither glanced at him. They stared at one another, a particular sort of anger mottling Kit's face and Townsend's body that Glennon was well acquainted with.

Glennon froze, feet rooting into the ground more out of habit than anything else. For some stupid reason, his body always tensed up when he walked into arguments, even if they didn't have a single thing to do with him. That sort of anger usually appeared in his dad's face and body *after* he'd raged, like when he'd been upset with Lee about the movies. Glennon always wished that expression would appear *before* the rage. It would be helpful in terms of preparing himself. That was the thing with anger though. Sometimes, there was no indication it was about to erupt.

"Hello, Glennon," Townsend said after a pause.

"Hey," Kit said.

Glennon wet his suddenly dry mouth and asked, "You know each other?"

"Oh no, we've only just met." Townsend reached up and pulled the hood of the black jacket she wore even farther over her brow. The jacket itself was an old, worn thing that looked like it'd been made a hundred years ago and had survived a thousand storms.

"I think we could be good friends though," Kit said.

"I have enough friends," Townsend said.

"You can always have more friends. Isn't that right, Glennon?" Kit asked.

Glennon's face twisted. "Uhh," he said, vocal cords freezing up as well. He didn't like walking into arguments, but he hated being dragged into the middle even more. If Kit and Townsend had only just met, how could they already be arguing?

"You only need enough friends to stop yourself from being lonely, and I'm not lonely," Townsend said. "I don't think Glennon is either."

Was he lonely? He hadn't a clue, but he did know that right now wasn't the time he wanted to figure it out.

"I like having friends," he said finally. "But not too many friends? Just the right number of friends. Enough friends. Friends are good. Good friends are good." *Good friends are good?* What was he even saying?

Both Townsend and Kit looked at him then.

"Are you okay?" Townsend asked.

No, he wasn't okay. His chest hurt. He was tired. He didn't want to be here. What he wanted was to go biking and not feel like something horrible was about to happen. He opened his mouth to lie and say, *I'm great,* when the shadows fell away from beneath Townsend's hood. In the same amount of time it took his heart to beat, her face took on the look of skin that was soggy with water, skin turning wrinkly and gray. It was almost as if his brain had dragged the drowned face he'd seen in the water moments before over Townsend.

But then the moment passed and her white skin was

smooth and tight over her cheeks, and her long black hair flowed over her shoulders.

Glennon's heart thrummed in his throat. He was definitely not okay.

"You're right," Kit said, dragging Glennon's focus away from Townsend. "Good friends are good."

"Yup," Townsend added. "Good friends *are* good."

Glennon forced one of his feet to obey his brain and take a step back. "I'm just…going to head back to the lighthouse now."

His other foot took a step as well. The feeling of *watchfulness* returned, of the monster lake holding its body still, in a state of forced calm. Shallow breaths filled his lungs, his breathing turning rapid in the same way Lee's often did after being yelled at.

"We might not be friends," Kit said, "but I think Glennon and I could be best friends. Best friends forever."

Kit was acting strange…but then he had reason to act oddly. He'd just survived a shipwreck, and he was probably still in shock. Glennon didn't know how long shock lasted, but it'd only been half a day since the accident.

All of a sudden, blinding whiteness crisscrossed Glennon's vision and leached into his chest. Lightning spanned the sky. It seemed to pierce through him, echoing inside the hurt place on his chest. He pressed the palm of his hand over his sternum and stared up at the quickly darkening sky.

Frizz and electricity filled the air. Freaked out by the lightning and the arguing pair and the pain in his bones, Glennon's knees unlocked and his legs carried out his orders to run.

"See you later, Glennon!" Townsend shouted after him.

He stumbled over the uneven rocks of the beach, and Graving Lighthouse came into view up the cliff. The eye at the top blinked on, lid peeling back to reveal the beam of light from its innards. Out it shone, casting its blazing ray into the day and pushing back the darkness that had leached over the sky.

Three days, Glennon thought. *Only three more days.*

He escaped toward Graving, needing every bit of its protection.

7

No more lightning shot through the clouds, though the sky turned
a peculiar shade of blue-black that reminded Glennon of art
class and paints and dirty water. His chest ached as he walked
up to the Third Keeper's house, almost as if a heavy sickness
tightened the cells of his lungs, except no cough rattled his
throat.

A shout erupted from somewhere inside the house when
he reached it—*Mom!*

He barreled into the living room to find her standing on
top of the armrest of the couch. She pointed one long, shaking
finger toward her feet. A rat stuck its sharp claws into the couch
and scrabbled up the fabric. There was something wrong with
it, with the way it moved and with the decaying fur on its back.
He dashed to the fireplace and grabbed up a long fire poker.

Glennon swatted at the rat and grazed its fur, dislodging it
from the couch. It toppled over and landed flat on its back. He
held the poker in the air, ready to ram it down on the rat's body

if it went for Mom again, but the rat didn't move. It lay still, no breath inflating its tiny body.

Had he killed it? He'd barely touched it!

"Isn't that strange." Mom crept off the couch, her stockinged feet leaving light imprints in the couch cushions.

The creature was little more than a skeleton. As they watched, the rat's body disintegrated. It folded in on itself, flattening in the middle and turning to dust around its edges. Mom bent over it, and so did Glennon, copying her. He held one hand over his nose to stop from breathing in the stink of death that seeped off the small body.

"I've never seen that happen before," Mom said. "It must've been sick with some strange disease. Don't touch it—" She held her arm out to him, even though he'd made no move to get close to the thing. "Get a mixing bowl from the kitchen."

He did as she instructed, grabbing one of the heavy bowls he'd seen Uncle Job use to mix biscuits the other morning. She dropped it over the rat, and then added a collection of other heavy objects on top of it, as if it might come back alive like one of Lee's zombie animals.

"We'll get Job to move it." She dusted her hands off.

"You're going to have to bleach the bowl later," Glennon said.

She laughed. "What, you don't want to eat out of a bowl that held a dead rat?"

Glennon gagged, and she laughed again.

"Where's your sister?" she asked, and he noticed then how pale her cheeks looked. The rat must have really scared her; it'd scared him too. "We need to head into town to buy a ferry ticket so that we can leave on the twentieth. Plus, we need groceries and new boots for you and your sister. I know you likely don't want to run errands, but remember that you can mail a letter to your father."

Glennon ran up the stairs. In his bedroom, he wedged his arm beneath the bed and dragged out the box with his notebook and stray sheafs of paper. As always, there were two piles he kept separate: the writing he hid away for himself and the writing he saved for his dad. He and his dad always wrote letters back and forth when his dad traveled, though sometimes it took a long time for Glennon to hear back—his dad was busy working.

"This atlas is all wrong," Lee said from the doorway. She wore the backpack sling still, the bottom hanging low with Seamus's weight.

"What?" Glennon asked, not looking up while he addressed an envelope.

"The atlas on your dresser. It has two dozen differ-ent pictures of Isle Philippeaux, but all of them are different shapes, and I've counted at least fifty-four lighthouses, but there definitely aren't fifty-four lighthouses that we've seen.

The lighthouses aren't even the same on all the drawings. Even Graving Lighthouse doesn't show up in all of them."

Glancing up, Glennon caught sight of the moleskin notebook. "That's the First Keeper's. Leave it alone."

She pushed the atlas across the dresser with one finger. "You're mailing a letter to Dad?"

"Course." He looked up, halfway through the process of licking the envelope. "Did you want to add a letter to mine?"

"I don't see the point. He doesn't respond."

"He responds."

"Not really. You write him pages and pages and all he sends back are pretty postcards."

"I like getting Dad's postcards. Just because Dad's mean to you and you don't want to write to him, doesn't mean that I don't." Glennon mashed his lips together, regretting what he'd said. Nobody ever talked about how mean their dad was to Lee. As a family, it was almost like they agreed to pretend it didn't happen.

Lee narrowed her eyes. "You think Dad's not mean to you too?"

He stood, shoving the envelope into his pocket, and then brushed by Lee, knowing it was better to stop the conversation altogether than try and argue his way around her.

Their mother already sat in the front seat of the car, engine running. The old Toyota Camry had been their grandma's, and even though it had nearly 200,000 miles on it, Mom refused to buy something new. Lee sat in the front, while Glennon took the back.

"What's wrong?" Glennon heard Lee ask, and he noticed Mom pressed one hand to her stomach.

"Acid reflux," Mom said, using an old person term just to say she had a stomachache. "I think breakfast this morning didn't agree with me."

Glennon heard Lee mention something about the movie *Aliens* then and promptly tuned out their conversation.

The road they drove curved through the island, at some points dipping into the forest and at others crossing close enough to the edge that it felt as if they were about to tip off into the water. He slid down in his seat and watched the lake blur by. Uncle Job had said before that the water was a measly thirty-five degrees, just above freezing, a temperature that could kill a man in minutes.

The road took a sharp curve along the coastline and headed into Shipyard Bay. There, massive ships maneuvered around one another with incredible care. The first time they'd visited the main town, Glennon had watched an enormous ship parallel park beside a loading station. He'd been very impressed.

There was no rational reason for it, but Isle Philippeaux felt wrong here, just as it did everywhere else. It reminded him of the feeling of an empty stomach, hollow and hungry.

Sometimes he wondered if the wrongness of this place was because the ships here made no sense. There were too many of them...or too many kinds. Wooden hulled ships, steamers, boats with big wheels rotating at their sides, and schooners with giant sails, like the pirate ship that appeared at the end of *The Goonies*.

They took a turn that brought them onto Main Street and had to slow to a crawl. The shipyard, when they'd passed it, had looked busy as always, and so too was Main Street. People teemed every which way, walking both on the sidewalk and straight down the center of the road, as if they didn't realize cars belonged there.

"Post office, Mom!" Glennon shouted, rising out of his seat, even though it made him feel exposed. She'd driven straight by the post office.

"You can walk. I'm parking in front of the grocery store." She slid the car into a parking spot.

Lee didn't head into the grocery store with Mom, but instead turned and walked down the middle of the street, saying, "I'm going down to the pier."

Seamus clawed his way out the backpack and draped his body over her shoulders, staring at the buildings and the people around him. His gaze locked on a woman who exited a yarn shop, her dress falling over her boots. It looked exactly like one of the dresses his sister had to wear when they'd had Prairie Days in elementary school.

A tiny bell rang above the door when he entered the post office. The postman on the other side of a counter turned from whatever task he was working on, a navy hat with a flat, glossy brim balanced on his head. It didn't look at all like the baseball cap the mail carrier wore back home.

Glennon slid his letter across the counter, saying, "I'd like one stamp, please."

"Course, young sir." The postman pulled a stamp off a sheet and stuck it on Glennon's envelope. "That'll be two cents, please."

Glennon frowned. It always confused him how cheap postage was here. Back home, they cost twenty-two cents and international postage was even more. He knew at some point in the past, they must've cost less than twenty-two, but not now.

Digging in his pocket, Glennon pulled out the quarter and nickel Mom had given him and passed the postman just the nickel. Getting three pennies in return, Glennon clutched them in his palm. Behind him, the bell over the door chimed and a woman entered.

She smiled at Glennon, then turned her attention to the man behind the counter. "Postman Ollie! Have my boxes arrived?"

"Sure have, Miss Lacey. Think you ordered some good books this time around?" Postman Ollie said.

"I've done my best. I ordered enough books to last us the next century!" She laughed, the light tinkling sound reminding Glennon of the bell above the door.

"Getting ready for The Waning, eh?"

"Always!"

Glennon couldn't control the way his muscles spasmed at hearing *The Waning*. Working to unlock his joints, he missed the rest of the conversation between Postman Ollie and Miss Lacey, right up until she said, "I haven't seen you around here before," and Glennon realized she was talking to *him*.

"I'm not a stranger here," he said, automatically. "My uncle is Job Johnson. He's Third—"

"Lighthouse Keeper at Graving Lighthouse. That would make you Glennon. I've heard about your visit to Graving. Everyone on the island has." Miss Lacey's expression shifted and some of the laughter that lined her eyes faded away. "I know your uncle well. He visits my library often."

"I didn't know he read," Glennon said.

"He loves to read, seems to prefer fantasy as a genre."

Surprise filled Glennon.

Miss Lacey's expression softened further. "You should ask him about it some time. Come visit me, if you ever need a book."

But then Postman Ollie came out from the back, pushing a cart filled with boxes. She reached out to touch the top of a box, and he noticed that on the back of her hand branched a series of red scars that stood out against her olive skin. The squiggly pattern of it reminded him of the lightning that had stretched across the sky earlier.

Glennon exited the post office before his brain could play tricks on him and *actually* make him see lightning, like it'd made him see Everett's face in the water.

"Go find your sister, please," Mom called from down the sidewalk. She was in the process of loading bags into the trunk of the car. "I'll start looking for boots for you both."

Glennon didn't bother complaining about having to find Lee, but he did pop the collar to his jacket and tuck his chin into the front, trying to turn himself invisible. He felt like eyes watched him from above, like someone peeked out from between the blinds in an upper story window to track his movement.

The shipyard was busy as always when he reached it. The ships made him feel tiny, like he was an ant staring up at the weathered vehicles of giants. He slipped between the chained gates of an iron fence that was meant to keep cars from entering the shipyard and, on the other side, spun straight into the chest of a man twice his size.

Glennon stumbled back. "So sorry," he said, pulling his jacket tight around his shoulders.

The man grabbed Glennon about the upper arms. His fingers dug into the soft skin there, pinching it uncomfortably. "*You.*"

Recognizing him, Glennon realized it was Gibraltar, the sailor who'd climbed the cliff with Everett and Kit.

The man bent low, eyes drawing near enough to Glennon's that he could count the streaks of amber that wove through his deep brown eyes. He opened his mouth, words trembling as they puffed out on a breath, and said, "*Please.* Have you figured out how to get off the isle?"

8

"Why do I need to get off the isle?" Glennon picked at the sailor's fingers, trying to peel off his grip.

"Why...*what*? Do you not—but..." The sailor's words turned gibberish, his pupils expanding. Glennon had seen Lee's eyes like that before, had seen Mom's eyes like that before...had even seen his own eyes like that, when staring into the mirror after being scared.

The sailor released Glennon, causing him to stumble.

"How can you stand the feel of it? How this island makes you *feel*?" Gibraltar pushed his fingers against his forehead. There, his skin stretched and swelled, right where the goose egg had grown the night before.

The dark purple streaks of a bruise showed beneath his skin. "We have to escape this place."

"It's an island. You can't just drive off it. You need a boat or something." Glennon immediately wished he could take back what he'd just said—the man was probably scared of boats considering he'd almost just died on one.

"No boats leave this place," he said.

"There are tons of boats!" Glennon pointed to the shipyard.

"But they never *leave*." Gibraltar didn't bother looking at the ships Glennon pointed to. "*Phantom ghosts on a phantom isle, they tie you down to stay a while,*" he chanted, almost as if he were singing.

Glennon had no idea what to say to Gibraltar's song. Obviously, the boats had to leave. "Why are you asking me how to get off the island? I'm a kid, and I've never looked up the ferry schedules."

Gibraltar bent down a little, then said, "We'll have to swim off."

"What? No! You can't swim in Lake Superior in December. You'd freeze!"

"It would be better than staying here though, no? *Shh.*" The sailor's eyes grew wary, narrowing as he glanced over Glennon's shoulder. "Shh. We'll have to talk later."

Talk later? Glennon didn't want to talk later.

"I won't let them catch me." Gibraltar hunched his shoulders, ducked his head, turned quick and escaped into the crowd that milled about the shipyard.

He disappeared fast enough that Glennon wondered if he'd really been there at all.

The cold of the shipyard flooded Glennon's senses, drying out his nose just like it was the very middle of winter. Quiet bootsteps approached behind him, and he turned to find Everett walking close, spine curved and eyes staring at Glennon in the same way Seamus stared at bugs before pouncing. He was ten thousand feet tall, warping massive and long, as if he'd stepped inside a fun house mirror and walked back out again, body elongated and strange.

Glennon blinked hard, trying to dislodge the vision. When he opened his eyes, Everett was just a few inches taller than him, the distorted view vanishing.

"Where did Gibby run off to?" Everett slung his arm over Glennon's shoulders, the white skin of his face pale and sickly against the watery gray sky behind him. "Gibby's been having a difficult time since the accident. He's been very confused and keeps running from me."

"He said something about wanting to swim off the island, but I think that would kill him." Glennon's body sagged, the bones inside his body feeling as if they were weighed down by stones instead of just Everett's arm.

"Sometimes surviving is more difficult than...not." Everett squeezed Glennon's neck with thumb and forefingers before letting go and shifting so he stood directly before him. "How have you been, Glen?"

Glennon paused, momentarily confused at who *Glen* was. No one called him Glen...except for his dad on odd occasions.

"I'm sure it was quite a shock to find us climbing up the side of your cliff," Everett said. "I hope you're recovering better than our Gibby."

"I'm okay." Glennon rubbed his face, trying to rid the insides of his nostrils of the feeling that he'd snorted the smoke of dry ice up his nose. It dribbled into his sinuses, filling his cheeks and forehead, and tunneled down his throat.

"Did you find Leeunah?" Mom shouted from somewhere behind Glennon.

"Hello, Miss Ruby," Everett called, not allowing Glennon to respond that *no,* he hadn't gotten the chance to find Lee.

"*Mrs.*" Mom walked through the chained gate.

Panic filled Glennon; he didn't want her getting close to Everett. Not at all.

"Glennon, did you find your sister?" Mom asked when she stood beside him. Her face—still, frozen, delicate and pristine and unbothered—held no emotions that Glennon could see.

"*Mrs.* Ruby," said Everett. "I apologize. I didn't realize you were married. I was under the impression that your husband had perhaps died."

"My dad's teaching overseas for a fellowship," said Glennon, defending his mom. His dad wasn't dead; he was just gone. There was a difference.

"I hope you're doing well after the trauma of last night."

Mom hooked one hand under Glennon's elbow and tugged in the direction of the pier where Lee had gone.

"I am, thank you." Everett stepped forward, entering Mom's personal space, standing within half-an-arm's reach. He took up all the air around Glennon, a ship in his own right, as if he were an empty steel vessel and something terrible and haunting rattled inside.

Glennon's mind exploded with sudden fear; he was drowning now, fully submerged, the icy melt of it flooding his chest. He couldn't breathe. *Protect Mom, keep her safe, help her,* whispered his mind.

"Let's go find Lee," he managed to say, then added, "She has Seamus."

At once, Everett's body stance shifted from attack to waiting—reminding Glennon of the long, invisible moment before his dad shouted inside the closed walls of their home. "Who is Seamus? I thought there were just three of you."

"Seamus is our cat," Glennon said. "He likes to watch the fish swimming off the pier."

"Your cat's here?" said Everett. The expanse of him faded, and Glennon realized he stood a body's length away, not half-an-arm's. "I don't like cats. I don't like the way they always seem to be thinking, and you never quite know what they're thinking about."

"I think cats are very nice," said Glennon, even though he wasn't always convinced that he did, in fact, like cats.

"It was lovely to see you again, *Mrs.* Ruby," Everett said, ignoring Glennon. "I hope we see one another again." He strode forward and took up Mom's hand, the pad of his thumb brushing against the skin along her palm.

Monster, screamed the voice inside Glennon. How was he failing so terribly at keeping Mom safe? Except...as Glennon stood still and tried to figure out what was happening, he couldn't quite pinpoint what was *wrong.* To any passerby, this moment would look like a normal one: three people standing on a sidewalk, having a nice chat. Two people shaking hands.

Everett's eyes met Glennon's over Mom's hand. There was a pause in time, a hiccup where the moment lengthened and everything inside Glennon squeezed into a place of stillness. It was as if he was being hunted and needed to stay frozen to avoid being consumed: a mouse trying to avoid an owl, a human trying to hide from a monster.

Glennon moved his own hand in slow motion. He reached out and gripped Mom's arm, physically pulling it from Everett.

Everett dropped her hand, then turned without saying goodbye and headed farther into the shipyard.

"I don't like him," Glennon said, watching him walk away.

"It's not nice to judge," said Mom.

The two of them walked in the same direction of Everett, though they did so at a much slower pace. They drew near the pier that jutted into the bay and that Lee had walked down. At the end of it was a small white house with a glowing light at the top. It was a lighthouse, albeit a much smaller one than Graving.

When they neared the start of the pier, Glennon took a last look at Everett. The man headed past a small, domed building at the edge of the shipyard. Lee liked that building, said it looked like a black marble because the entire thing was made of dark glass that the staff inside made sure to keep well shined.

In the glass, Glennon watched passersby bob and sway as they walked along the curve of the bay and the shipyard.

Reflected in the glass, too, was the image of white clouds in the sky, a massive ship that entered the yard, seagulls wheeling over the water, and a streak of dissipating fog right over the walkway. It hovered beside where Everett was supposed to be, but in the mirror, there was no Everett, there was only fog and the creeping sense of dread. A stiff wind blasted over the bay and all at once, the mist broke up and wafted away, disappearing entirely, leaving the reflection empty of anyone.

Glennon's mind swum through the feeling of a nightmare, of trying to catch up with reality. He turned to the actual image of Everett. The man stood exactly where he should, exactly where he *didn't* stand in the mirror.

Everett stopped all of a sudden. He turned, slow. Facing Glennon, he raised one hand, and then waved, his fingers twiddling, playing the piano midair more than waving goodbye to Glennon. Except this too only existed in reality and not at all in the mirrored glass behind him.

Monster? said Glennon's brain, confused.

Something twitched within the pocket on Everett's jacket, right over his heart. Two glowing eyes peeked free, then two clawed paws. A rat, the same sort of mangy creature that had attacked Mom earlier and that had sat on her windowsill during the night. It climbed out and perched on Everett's shoulder, almost as if it were a parrot and Everett were a pirate. It stared at Glennon in just the same way that Everett stared.

"Three days," Glennon whispered to himself. All they had to do was survive another three days, then they would be free of this place.

9

"The ferry isn't running," Mom said to Glennon.

"What?" he said.

"I tried to buy a ticket, but the ticket master said the ferry was gone. It seems a hoard of rats got into the engine and chewed up the cables. It's no longer running. A tugboat towed it to Duluth to have it fixed, and it won't return for quite a while."

Rats? What was it with this island and rats? "But...how will we leave? We're supposed to go in three days."

"I'm not sure, Glennon."

"Can we take a different boat?"

"The ferry is the only one equipped to transport our car."

"So?"

"You want me to leave Grandma's car here?"

Yes! screamed a voice inside Glennon. Anything to get off the island and away from Everett and away from his rats and away from The Waning...whatever The Waning actually was.

The memory of Gibraltar's voice crawled up Glennon's

spine: *Have you figured out how to get off the isle? We have to escape this place.*

Mom's gaze shifted past Glennon. Her head listed toward one side, and her mouth opened. She sang a little, even though she hated singing when people could hear. *"Later that night when 'is lights went outta sight came the wreck of the* Edmund Fitzgerald."

Mom motioned at the bay and the ship that'd sailed in. It was a long freighter, and music piped from somewhere inside its hull, echoing throughout the bay.

"It's lyrics of a song by Gordon Lightfoot, about the *Edmund Fitzgerald*, a ship that sunk in the mid-70s. I remember reading news clippings about it." She hummed a little more of the song. "It's funny, don't you think, that they would name another ship the *Edmund Fitzgerald*, considering the first sunk?" She pointed to the freighter and the name *Edmund Fitzgerald* was stamped across its front.

The ship stole through the bay, and for a moment, its image warped in the same way Everett had. The white and brown behemoth turned soft and green with moss. Icicles made of rust dripped from its railing, and a massive crack appeared in its middle, almost like the break in the *Anabeth*. But as soon as Glennon's brain registered what it saw, the image disappeared, turning once again into the immaculate, unbroken freighter.

Mom hummed some more, then sang, "*Superior,' they said, 'never gives up her dead when the gales of November come early.'*"

⁓

Glennon raced down the pier toward his sister. Mom trailed slowly behind.

"Why are you running?" asked a voice to Glennon's right.

Skidding, Glennon came to a halt. Just below the pier ran a layer of cement that sat close to the water's surface, almost like a step down toward the water. There, a few fishermen stood with lines bobbing in the lake, and standing among them was Kit.

Glennon's brain hurt. He'd *just* seen Kit halfway across the isle. "How did you get here? You were just at Graving!"

"You were just at Graving too," Kit said, frowning.

"My mom brought me here in her car. You don't have a car."

"Townsend has a boat though." In the distance, a small boat zoomed across the water.

"Oh," Glennon said, confused. He had thought Kit and Townsend weren't friends. He'd also thought Kit was supposed to be with Everett—shouldn't they be getting checked out by a doctor or something after the accident? Trying to be nice even though he was in a hurry, he asked, "Caught any fish?"

"Not yet. I'm not really any good at fishing. It looks like I'll be on the island for a while, though, so I figured I might as well try my hand at it."

"Oh, you can't leave either? Were you supposed to take the ferry too?"

"What?"

"The ferry. My mom said the ferry was sent to Duluth for repairs. We're going to have to find another way off the isle." Kit probably needed the ferry to take him to his family who surely was waiting for him somewhere on the edge of Superior.

Sadness flickered around Kit's eyes, making something deep in Glennon feel sad too. "Yeah. I can't leave."

"I'm sorry." Glennon stepped backward, needing to get to Lee. He felt bad for Kit though—maybe his family could get a fisherman to bring them to Isle Philippeaux. "Are you staying at Uncle Job's house again tonight?"

"Am I invited?" Kit asked, sounding hopeful. "I'm not sure where else I'm supposed to go."

"Of course," Glennon said, feeling awful the adults on the island hadn't worked harder to help Kit. Shouldn't the keepers or Everett or someone find him a place to stay?

"Thank you." Kit tugged on his fishing pole. The end popped out of the water, and a bundle of weeds flew out. Among the mess were the remains of a fish, tiny bones poking free from the scales.

"I have to go find my sister." He pointed his thumb at the

end of the pier, his gaze stuck on the fish carcass a moment too long. A knot formed in his stomach thinking of all the dead things in the lake.

"I'll see you later!" Kit waved, and Glennon took the opportunity to run again.

He found Lee standing beneath the small white lighthouse at the end of the pier. It was lofted in the air on ten-foot-high stilts with a white iron ladder leading to its door. Seamus sat beside her, the floofy gray hair on his tail blowing in the wind as he peered over the edge of the cement and into the water lapping below.

"Lee!" Glennon shouted. "I have an important question."

Lee didn't look up, but Seamus did. The cat glared at Glennon, as if Glennon had just ruined a very nice moment between him and Lee.

"Lee. Please. It's important." Glennon walked beneath the little house and swallowed hard against the terror that wedged inside his throat. "Do monsters have reflections?"

"I would assume so," Lee said. "Monsters have mass and form. Most things with mass and form have reflections, unless they're invisible."

"Can monsters be invisible?"

"Probably. Depending on the type or on how their biology works. They could have skin that could turn invisible or camouflage them, like chameleons."

"But…could a monster that's visible not have a reflection? The monster itself is visible but the reflection is invisible?"

Lee glanced away from the water. "What are you talking about? I need more information to give you a real answer."

A small part of Glennon didn't want to admit what he was thinking, but a bigger part of him didn't want Mom hurt. He was intensely grateful Lee was here, because she took his questions seriously. If Dad stood before him, there was no way Glennon could ask him anything about monsters. "I just saw Everett standing before the black glass house. He stood outside it, but his reflection didn't show in the mirrors. I'm trying to figure out what sorts of creatures wouldn't have a reflection."

"Vampires," Lee said.

"Everett can't be a vampire though!" Glennon shoved the palms of his hands against his eyes, his heart doing a dance inside his chest that made his body feel sick. "Vampires aren't real! Dad would say so."

"Dad doesn't know everything in the whole wide world."

It feels like it. Dropping his hands, Glennon wondered if it was true that there were limits to their dad's knowledge. He certainly talked like he knew everything.

Lee's eyes glittered like Lake Superior, brightening with the talk of monsters. "Everett could be a vampire. We haven't seen him in daylight. Vampires can't be outside in the sun."

"I saw him just now. He didn't burn up."

Lee pointed toward the slate-gray sky. "The sun isn't really *out*."

She was right. The sun hadn't made a full appearance since that morning. It still looked as if the day wanted to storm.

"Can vampires come out on cloudy days?" He asked.

"If Everett's a vampire, then I'd say...yes." Lee grinned.

"It's not funny!" Glennon burst out. "You weren't there just now. You weren't there when Everett grew ten feet and didn't have a reflection and got too close to Mom. He's magical, I swear! Something's wrong with him, and I don't think Mom can tell. She told me not to judge him when I said I didn't like him."

Lee stopped laughing. She considered him in the same serious way she did when she talked about movies with her friends. "You don't believe in magic."

Glennon's body held too many emotions; he wanted to stomp his feet like he used to when he was a little kid. "It doesn't matter what I believe. I know what I saw."

"Do you believe what you saw?"

Pausing with his mouth open, the fear that had ridden on his chest for the last ten minutes clambered onto his shoulders. He drooped beneath it. What was it their dad always said to Lee...about her wild imagination and how it infected her rational thought?

Glennon didn't want to have more things be wrong with him. He was already stupid; he didn't want to add *making things up* to the list of bad things about himself. What if everything he'd seen and felt in the last day had been his brain making things up?

Don't believe every ridiculous thing your brain tries to tell you, he pictured his dad saying.

"I believe something's wrong," Glennon whispered, not quite able to believe in himself entirely.

"Close enough! I've been *waiting* for someone else to admit something creepy is happening on this isle." She talked so fast, she interrupted his bad thoughts and didn't give him time to question himself. "The entire place is a confusing mess, and no one will give me straight answers when I ask about why."

His sister scooped Seamus into her arms. The cat meowed, voice dipping low, as if to say, *But I was having fun!*

Glennon stumbled after her, as she hurried in Mom's direction. He tried to keep up both with his feet and with his mind. "Where are we supposed to start searching for answers about Everett?"

"The place we begin is *vampires,*" Lee said, as if it was the most logical thing in the world.

10

"You two look thick as thieves," Mom said on the drive back to the lighthouse.

Glennon and Lee both sat in the back seat, their heads close together as they whispered while Mom listened to the radio. Mom was right. They had never been siblings who were best friends or who spent a ton of time together. They were more like frequent acquaintances who passed in the hall and sometimes bothered to ask how the other was doing. Now, though, they probably looked like they were concocting some sort of plan...which they were.

Mom ended up buying boots and telling them, "If you don't like them, you're stuck with them until you grow and need new ones."

She pressed two fingers to her temple and massaged. The skin beneath her eyes had a dark sheen to it, looking more purple and puffy than white and smooth, almost exactly how it looked when she woke after crying the night before.

"Are you alright?" Lee asked.

"I'm feeling tired," said Mom. "I might need a nap."

"You never take naps," Glennon said.

Mom met his gaze in the rearview mirror. He glanced away, wishing he hadn't said anything. He felt like he always said the wrong things when what he wanted was to help. "I'm going to take a nap when we get to Job's. While I do so, it would be smart for you two to take a look at the homeschool work you have for tomorrow."

Both Glennon and Lee groaned. They turned away from one another and sunk into their seats.

"No complaining. This was part of the deal of coming up here."

The "deal" of coming to Isle Philippeaux for the months their dad was gone was that they would be homeschooled, since they were being pulled out of regular class. Lee and Glennon were eleven months apart in age, and one year apart in school, and being homeschooled was never their choice; it was always just what Mom chose for them.

Back at the Third Keeper's house, Mom dumped the shopping bags on the staircase and pressed her hand tight to her chest. Glennon watched as she headed up the stairs, his hand floating to his own sternum, where the dull thump of pain still registered.

Lee stared after Mom. "Everett didn't actually *bite* her, did he? She never takes naps, and she never *doesn't* put away groceries. She's too organized, always says we put things in the wrong places."

"No biting occurred," Glennon confirmed. He dropped his hand from his bruised ribcage and picked up a shopping bag. He was convinced Everett had done something to Mom, he just wasn't sure what. Whatever it was, though, it'd made her worn out. Her skin had looked nearly translucent.

Glennon and Lee argued about how to put away the groceries, trying their best to organize the cans of Campbell's soup, and then returned to the front door where Mom had set the bag containing the boots. Lee fished inside the bag. She pulled her boots out and stared hard. They were blue Moon Boots with red and yellow stripes across the middle.

Glennon pulled his out as well; they had the exact same pair.

"She made us match?" Lee said.

"These went out of style years ago… She did warn us that we were stuck with them." Glennon tugged on the boots. They were toasty warm inside and comfortable when he stood, even if they did make it look as if he were walking with blue clouds stuck to his feet. "At least we can take the liners out and use them for slippers."

"I kind of like them," Lee said.

"You *would* like wearing vinyl Moon Boots. Weirdo."

Lee giggled, and Glennon laughed with her. The handle to the front door rattled, and all at once, it popped open. Deep shadows filled the doorway and a large shadow filled every inch of the threshold.

Both Glennon and Lee stopped laughing.

"I am going to light a bonfire," Uncle Job said as he stepped into the entryway and held up a log.

Glennon let out a gusty breath. He hadn't recognized Uncle Job at first, which was confusing, considering the fact that Uncle Job was pretty distinctive.

"Something about the warmth of firelight always puts my worries at ease," Uncle Job said. "Seems too that we should make use of what's probably the last nice weather day for the next six months."

Lee followed Uncle Job out the door, with Seamus still strapped to her chest in her backpack. She grabbed a flashlight as she went.

"Take earplugs," Uncle Job said, his low voice carrying far without him having to talk louder. It was a voice that calmed something inside Glennon. "Keep them in your pockets in case the fog rolls in tonight. No need to ruin your hearing at such a young age. You have high school and college for that, with all the parties and concerts you're sure to go to."

Lee snorted, but she doubled back for the earplugs that were stored on the table beside the door. Glennon shoved a pair into his pocket as well. Together, they followed Uncle Job into the late afternoon.

It was an hour before dinner, but this far north, the sky had already turned midnight blue, especially since chalky clouds covered the sinking sun. Graving Lighthouse's light spilled out over Superior with its steady rhythm going *on-off, on-off, on-on-off.*

Uncle Job's quiet steps led them away from the keepers' houses and toward the cliff. Glennon looked to the water, and he found that the *Anabeth* no longer hovered atop the rock. Either the coast guard had towed the broken ship away, or it'd slipped into the graveyard below. They headed to the left, to the top of the stairs that led to the beach. A nice clearing was kept there, along with a stone bonfire pit and logs for stools.

Uncle Job dropped the wood he carried. The logs thumped against the ground, and Glennon flinched at the unexpected sound, a shot of adrenaline coursing through him. He'd never liked unexpected, sharp noises; they always reminded him of the sound of a fist punching a wall.

Still, be still, Glennon told himself. His body had no reason to make him feel afraid of Uncle Job, but that's exactly what he'd felt when the logs had hit the ground.

Uncle Job frowned at Glennon, asking, "You alright?"

"Umm," Glennon said, at a loss. His entire body felt like one big bruise. Sure, he still ached from falling off his bike, but that wasn't it—he felt bruised *inside* himself, though he couldn't quite pinpoint the origin of the internal punch.

Lee eyed Glennon, then said into the silence that had stretched into awkwardness, "Glennon had a spooky day. He's feeling a bit like a raw nerve." She patted him on the shoulder.

Uncle Job grunted and bent down. He placed logs inside the stone ring and then kindling inside that.

Lee leaned close to Glennon's ear and said, "Usually I'm the one to be jumpy at loud noises. What's wrong with you?"

"I've had a spooky day," Glennon whispered back, repeating her words.

Thin, hollow steps came out of the darkness. Uncle Job didn't look up, but Glennon's whole body peeled away from the direction the sound came, and he jerked his flashlight toward the top of the staircase. A head appeared, hidden inside a dark hood.

"Is it bonfire time?" The shadows beneath Townsend's hood didn't disappear, even with Glennon's flashlight shining on her.

His empty fist clenched. He wanted to see her face, even though he knew it was ridiculous—he knew if he looked at her, he wouldn't find the skin of a drowned person.

Behind Townsend, another head appeared up the stairs. *Kit!* He was much quieter than Townsend, his steps muffled against the wooden stairs. Townsend must have given him another ride across the lake, so he could spend the night at Uncle Job's house. Glennon waved, and Kit waved back, grinning.

Light bloomed in the darkness, Uncle Job's fire taking hold of the kindling and blazing into existence. Warmth hit Glennon's face and soaked into his skin. It pushed away some of the worry rooted inside his bones.

"I'll leave you kids to it." Uncle Job placed his hands on his knees and levered himself up. His head blocked out the moon when he stood.

"But you didn't get to enjoy the fire," Glennon said, feeling like they'd forced Uncle Job away.

"You didn't get to put your worries at ease," Lee added.

Uncle Job hesitated. He glanced at Townsend and Kit, then back at Glennon and Lee. "Plenty of time for that later."

"But not until winter's over—you said it's probably the last nice weather day for the next six months," Glennon said.

Uncle Job waved away Glennon's words and headed back toward the keepers' houses. "Perhaps I'll make dinner tonight. It seems like a good evening for tomato soup and grilled cheese."

Glennon watched Uncle Job walk into the evening, the gentle movement of his footfalls at contrast with his huge body.

Before disappearing, Uncle Job spoke into the darkness. "Since you're here, Townsend, you should tell a ghost story."

"You know a ghost story?" Lee sunk onto one of the logs that surrounded the fire. She leaned forward, squishing Seamus in his backpack. He squirmed and she undid the zipper, letting him climb out and onto the grass. "I love ghost stories."

Townsend sat opposite the fire, her jacket still buttoned tight around her. The flames painted her chin with light and lit the undersides of her hood, though dark shadows still covered her face. "I know many ghost stories, but—" She drummed her fingers against the log she sat on, the thumps filling the silence between cracks of the fire. "The one I think I should tell is about *here*."

Lee trembled with excitement. Glennon trembled too, though for an altogether different reason. He was already dealing with vampires; why did he have to deal with ghosts now too?

Seamus picked up his paws one at a time, seeming to not like the cold, brittle grass beneath them. Glennon shook his head at the spoiled cat and reached out. For the first time in days, Seamus didn't hiss when Glennon picked him up. He tucked Seamus onto his lap, and Seamus butted his head against the middle of Glennon's chest, making the bruise hurt. Glennon turned Seamus around and stuck his fingers into the cat's warm fur for comfort.

Townsend held out her arms toward Graving. "People say that this lighthouse is named thus because a small shipyard was once built here, and a graving dock is another name for a shipyard. That's a nice story, but that's all it is—a nice story, and it's not the *real* story."

Kit settled himself on the log beside Glennon. The place where Kit sat became a blur of darkness at his periphery, almost as if the fire were playing a trick on his vision and obscuring Kit from his view. When he looked directly at Kit, though, he smiled. Glennon smiled back. As soon as he faced Townsend, the blur returned.

Just a trick of the fire, Glennon told himself, and he stopped thinking about it as Townsend continued.

Her voice lowered, turning resonant, as if she spoke from inside a deep, damp cavern. "Welcome to the story of Graving Lighthouse, and how it got its name."

11

Long ago, the haunted remains of humans were rumored to walk
Superior's depthless waters—

"I already don't like this story." Glennon held Seamus tight.

"*Shhh.*" Lee shoved her finger in his face.

Glennon swatted his hand at Lee's and then rolled his eyes
at Kit. Kit grinned and rolled his eyes too. He leaned close and
whispered, "I like adventure stories better than ghost stories.
They're more fun."

Glennon agreed.

Lee pulled off her backpack and shoved it at Glennon.
Glennon wrinkled his nose, but not knowing what else to do
with it, he stuck his arms through the loops, and sure enough,
Seamus climbed right in.

Townsend slipped back into her storytelling voice, and
the world around Glennon dimmed. Her voice muted the light
breeze on his ears and the hard log beneath his thighs and the
swish of water in the distance.

Back then, ships were made of wood instead of steel and captains navigated by sextant and instinct. Lake Superior's maps were imprecise, made more by guesswork and written records of travelers than by land surveys and precise images taken from the air. Sailors had to be careful, for it was already well known that Lake Superior, with its uncertain tides and unpredictable weather, was a tomb for ghosts.

The problem with ghosts is that they're not so easy to ward off when you've stepped into their territory. Lake Superior was claimed by the dead, and when the living sailed onto its waters, they risked becoming one of the dead as well.

A shudder clambered out of Glennon's chest and straight through his arms. He'd been on that creepy water before.

Superior is not like the ocean with its salty waters and swimming beasts that consume bodies, or like the earth beneath us in which humans bury people, allowing them the chance to decay. Superior is a watery grave that preserves the dead, and it's partly this preservation that keeps ghosts' spirits aloft.

Our tale begins somewhere along Superior's coastline, with a sailing crew and their ship, newly lightened and floating easy upon the lake, for they'd recently docked to unload the ore they carried. A terrible storm had ransacked the lake the day before, turning it into a froth of twenty-foot waves and terrible whirls of wind. On this day, though, the captain peered into the creamy sky with its buttery-smooth clouds and decided it was safe to sail—you know, once a storm has passed, it is long gone…never to return.

Glennon's breathing turned shallow. It was never a good thing when a story said something like *never to return*. That practically promised it would come back. He scooted forward on the log. Beside him, Kit did as well.

Seeing as it was November, the most perilous month in which to sail, the crew was eager to return to their home port under good sailing conditions. There, they would leave their ship and head home to wait out the wintry months. The day was beautiful and bright, with fall sunshine turning the lake into sparkling crystal. But as November tends to go, the storm they thought had disappeared, returned.

"Knew it," Glennon muttered.

It was as if the storm of the previous day had been tossed back over Superior by a giant. It slingshotted across the lake. The twenty-foot waves transformed into forty-foot towers of water; the terrible whirls of wind now whooshed into gales that ripped sailcloth and rope to shreds. The crew no longer knew their location on the lake. Amid the heaving, icy water, they were lost.

The fire before Glennon tumbled over itself. Blue and red tongues of flame bashed into the logs, waves churning against wood and burying it beneath ash.

The captain shouted orders to his men, directing them through the storm. His confidence settled their nerves. He was as seasoned a sailor as any of them, and he would keep them safe.

But as they sailed, the men became consumed with dread. The captain tried to keep them focused, but one by one, they became convinced something walked inside the storm itself, that perhaps the storm wasn't true weather at all. Perhaps it was the making of ghosts, meant to drag them all beneath the waves. One sailor, a man who'd worked under the captain for near a dozen years, stood on the deck, unable to move. He'd made the mistake of listening to the howls of the wind. Sobbing, he shouted to his captain, "I hear the dead. They need life. They starve!"

The captain wrestled the sailor below deck, yelling at him to stay calm. Back above, the rest of the crew succumbed to the shrieks in the wind as well.

The sailor who'd gone below deck had wrapped his head inside his shirt, buffeting his ears against the haunted murmurings of the phantoms. The sailor calmed, as he could no longer hear what the ghosts said. He headed back to the pounding waters above deck with his ears plugged tight. There, he found the entire crew dismantled. Everyone cried, begging the captain not to let the dead eat their souls…but the captain was nowhere to be found.

Glennon pressed the pads of his fingers to his cheeks and placed his feet on the stone of the firepit. He tried to get his toes away from the ground, away from the feeling that water sloshed beneath him.

The sailor scoured the deck best he could in the storm, clinging to rope and wood and men's arms when needed, and there! He spotted the captain moving easily across the deck, as if the water was made of smoke. The sailor chased him down, skittering over the deck that had turned slippery with water and blood.

"Captain!" shouted the sailor. He pulled from his ears the earplugs and the shirt so he could hear the captain's response. What are we to do? The men have given in to the siren's song of the dead!

"We are headed to the lighthouse. Its light will show us the way home." The captain raised his arm and pointed into the distance. There, a sudden light blinked into existence. The sailor watched the light churn against the storm, the on-off, on-off, on-on-off beat as if it were trying to push away the darkness. He turned to thank the captain, but the captain had disappeared.

And all at once the sailor knew that even if they headed toward safety, it would be impossible to dock in a storm such as this. The ship was bound to run straight into the lighthouse itself...or whatever it was the lighthouse stood up on. Frantic, the sailor threw himself at the captain's wheel, trying to turn them away from the cliffs that came into view. Except there, he collapsed in a despairing heap, because he found the captain's body bumping against the massive ship's wheel that he'd tied his body to.

The captain's body was in ruins. To be in such a state, he must've

*been dead for quite some time. If this was the captain and his body,
then who was it the sailor had spoken to moments before?*

Glennon stared at Townsend. At the hood that hid her face,
the eerie firelight that glowed against the bottom of her chin, the
deep shadows that covered her eyes. Her fingers hovered in the air,
painting pictures that Glennon swore he could see. He saw each
stroke of them—the dead captain at the wheel, the broken ship
beneath them, the raging storm around them…the lighthouse
just out of reach. He looked away and into the fire. Fuzzy black
images appeared the longer he stared.

*Dread suffocated the sailor. The feeling poured from a spot
directly behind him, and he knew that when he looked, he would
find the ghost. He turned.*

*"I told you. I'm starving," said the ghost who still wore the
body of the captain. The image melted away, the ghost transforming
into a being made of wind and water, with debris swirling in its
innards. It was made of the storm itself. "I am not without hospital-
ity; let me welcome you to my home."*

*As the sailor watched, the squall thinned. A lighthouse stood at
the edge of a tall, sharp cliff. At its base were dozens upon dozens of
ship carcasses. They littered the lake floor and so too did the bones of
sailors.*

Glennon couldn't look away from the fire, from the
dark images that rotated in the flames. Inside them, Graving

Lighthouse took shape, and so too did the cliff, the graveyard of ships, the dead sailors.

The ship crashed straight into the rocks of the cliff. Above the wreck rotated Graving's light, promising warmth and safety... promising a new home. Townsend's voice rose to a crescendo. *The ghost had driven them all straight into the face of death!*

Flames in the fire licked together and curved into the shallow-cheeked shape of a skull. The bones of the forehead glistened with icy heat. Flat teeth grinned at Glennon. Death stared straight into his soul.

Glennon shoved away from fire and fell off the log. Seamus, in the backpack, fell right along with Glennon and landed on his chest. Kit shouted and tried to grab for Glennon as he scrambled away.

The face inside the fire gaped at him, jaw peeling apart to reveal black hunger inside. Rage and misery flooded the caverns of its eye sockets, ghosting up the image of Glennon's dad mid-fury, mid-destruction, mid-*why do I have such an incompetent son!*

Glennon's body usually froze when it was confronted with something scary, like his dad, but this time, his mind said *run*.

And so, he ran.

12

Glennon's awareness narrowed to only the motions of his body: feet thumping, knees hinging, elbows swinging, lungs bellowing, and forearms turning into battering rams that broke branches and bushes. He pummeled straight through the woods, snapping twigs off trees and kicking rocks out of the way and stubbing his toes on roots.

Seamus's backpack thumped hard against his chest, sending shockwaves of pain through his ribcage. Inside the bag, Seamus stayed quiet, though his nails ripped through the canvas cloth and into Glennon's jacket.

He meant to run for Graving, but somehow, in his terror, he'd entered the woods and now, he couldn't seem to get out. Nothing looked familiar, though he *knew* the gravel road had to be close. He should be able to see the lighthouse!

He shot through the skeletal forest, flashlight swinging. The beam carved a path through the woods. The yellowing light turned wild in his hand just like the flames of the fire had turned confusing. It jumped and wiggled across the forest, like tiny maggots squirming across the white bones of the trees. He screamed, dropping the light.

How, how, how, whimpered his mind as he galloped between two trees, narrowly grown together. His bruised hip bumped one trunk and his foot caught against the other, and he fell head over heels. He came upright, his legs straight in front of him as momentum carried him forward into a full stretch, forehead nearly touching his knees and fingers ringing his heels.

He sat that way, his body hunched and trembling, short breaths panting out through his nose. Where was Graving? Why couldn't he find the lighthouse? How had the woods gotten so confusing? How was it possible that the ghost from Townsend's story had invaded the fire? Worse, why did his brain have to make the ghost look like his dad?

"Stupid brain." Glennon knocked his knuckles against his head. "Stupid, stupid brain."

Seamus meowed, startling Glennon. The cat hissed and scrabbled at the innards of the backpack.

"I'm sorry." Glennon undid the zipper, and Seamus flew out.

The cat faced him with his back arched. His fur stood on end, turning him into a snarling porcupine.

"I didn't mean to run. I didn't mean to run and take you

with me. Usually you're with Lee and not me, anyway." Glennon spread his hands wide. "I'm not a very good cat brother."

Seamus tiptoed away from Glennon, all the while keeping his wide-eyed gaze locked on him.

"I'm sorry, okay?" Glennon said, a bit desperate. Seamus had never been this mad at him before.

Glennon climbed to his feet, one hand pressed flat against his chest. It felt as if the terrible bruise on his bone had spread all over him, deepening from his sternum straight through to his spine. Taking a moment to gather himself, he was surprised to find that even without the flashlight, he could see well enough. Moonlight glowed around them, the moon itself a day or so away from being full. It highlighted the blades of grass in every dip and knoll of the clearing he'd run into.

Far off in one corner of the glade where trees grew tall, the broken remains of a stone building lay half-buried and crumbling. He grabbed up the flashlight he'd dropped and shone it over its broken stones.

He took a step toward it, but as he did, he tripped over an uneven place in the grass and landed hard on his knees. Glaring at the place he'd fallen, he noticed a small flat stone. Silver light from the moon struck the wedged imprints of letters on the rock, all capital and unevenly carved.

CHRISTOPHER PICARD

1802–1816

LIVED WELL. DIED TERRIBLY.

Breath stilled in his chest. Glennon pinched his eyes shut and tried not to think about the fact that he'd clearly landed atop someone's *tomb*.

"Don't run," he hissed to himself, even though his body desperately wanted to send him on another flailing, terrified escape through the woods. "A graveyard is just a graveyard, even when it's on a creepy island."

Slowly, he stood. He beckoned to the Seamus. "We need to leave. I know you're mad at me, but you gotta get back into the backpack."

"Who are you talking to?"

Glennon jumped, both flinching and freezing at the same time. He turned and found Kit standing in the center of the crumbled building—the *church*. It had to be a church. Didn't graveyards usually have churches? He pointed at the stone foundation and whispered, "You shouldn't stand in there. It's probably haunted," not caring at *all* that right now he sounded exactly like Lee, overly imaginative and irrational. His dad would be so mad.

Kit set his hands on his hips and looked about the stones and the platform. Then, smiling, teeth reflecting moonlight, he did a little jig in the center of the church.

"Ugh! Stop." Glennon covered his eyes, but then he laughed, and tension spooled out of him. Kit looked ridiculous. "You shouldn't dance."

"It made you stop being so paranoid, though, didn't it?" Kit stepped over the broken wall and walked toward Glennon.

"You wish." The relief that had washed through him when he laughed disappeared as he watched Kit step right on top of a divot in the grass. "Don't—*don't* walk over here. There are dead people under there."

"Wouldn't they be dead *bodies*? The word 'people' seems to imply they're still alive somehow."

"It's not funny!" Glennon whisper-shouted. He refused to give in to the temptation and actually shout; he had no desire to wake up whatever existed in this place. "How did you find me? I got turned around and couldn't find Graving."

"Your path through the woods wasn't hard to follow," Kit said.

Glennon ducked his head, embarrassed. There were probably broken tree branches and snapped twigs all through the forest now. "I bet Lee was mad I ran away before Townsend finished her story."

Kit shrugged. "Who cares about Townsend's story. It's just a story. Sorry you got scared."

I wasn't scared, Glennon wanted to say, even though that

was ridiculous. Obviously he'd been freaked out. What he could say though was "The *story* didn't scare me."

"Something did."

"The…" He lost his words. He couldn't exactly pinpoint what had made him the most scared: seeing the face in the fire or feeling his dad's unexpected presence before him. Both were terrifying. He reached over then to try and pick up Seamus, but the cat shot away into the woods. His hands closed around air. "This is a graveyard, and I found the worst tombstone. *Sorry*," he said to whoever Christopher Picard was. He didn't mean to insult the dead.

"Which one?"

Glennon pointed. "It says *lived well, died terribly*. Who would write something that awful on a gravestone?"

"Someone with a sense of humor. The graveyards on Isle Philippeaux aren't exactly known for their ability to give the dead rest." Kit bent to peer at the inscription on the stone. "You should visit some of the other cemeteries sometime. You'll see what I mean. Lots of gallows humor, awful as it is. This isn't my first time on this island, you know. I've been here before."

It made sense that Kit had been on the island before; it explained why he knew his way around so well. Glennon knew about gallows humor from Lee. She said people sometimes made jokes in scary movies when terrible things were happening.

Looking away from Kit, he concentrated back on the tombstone. What little light existed faded, until only the tombstone came into focus. Everything around it, even Kit, disappeared behind a black fuzz, a hole that felt gaping and empty. The air cooled and his heart ached. The whole world felt as if it were lacking something important, something necessary, almost as if he stood before the tombstone of a person he'd loved. Except…he obviously didn't know Christopher Picard. Why should he feel sad looking at the grave of a person he didn't know?

He reached out a hand, feeling the air, and realized that the sadness didn't come from *inside* him, it came from *outside*. It existed in the air itself, and the longer he stood in its presence, the more it seeped into his body—it oozed out of the graveyard and straight into his bruised bones.

Something haunted this place.

"What's wrong?" Kit asked.

Glennon snatched his hand back and stepped away. "Do you know how to get back to the lighthouse?"

Kit hesitated. He glanced about him and the shallow depressions that pockmarked the earth. Wispy mist rolled through the grass around his feet, moonlight turning the meadow into a smudge of color, more white and blue than green and brown.

A low beat of pain crept up Glennon's spine and lodged firmly between his eyes. "I want to go home."

"Home to the lighthouse?" Kit drifted toward him. "The same home as Townsend's ghost?"

"Please stop with the ghost stories," he said, refusing to care how pathetic he sounded.

"It's okay to be scared of ghost stories." Kit's voice floated in the air, coming from all directions.

"I'm not scared," Glennon whispered.

The misery inside the cemetery, inside the air above the graves, leaked through Glennon's body and dripped into the cavern of his chest. Dread pooled in the seams of his lungs. The hurt in his breastbone contracted his vision into a small slit.

Kit sighed, a great lofty breath that for a moment cleared the blur from Glennon's vision. Kit pulled Glennon's arm over his shoulder and hooked his own around Glennon's chest, right where the pain looped around his ribcage.

"Yeah," Kit said, quiet. "I know the way back to your home."

Kit's strength carried Glennon through the woods and back toward Graving, leaving the graveyard behind in the middle of the woods. Glennon vowed never to return.

13

Glennon woke early the next morning and sat beside the window to write, his mind ticking a silent *two days, two days, two days.* They had to find a way off the island. He didn't want to have to stay any longer than they'd been promised, and they'd always planned to leave in two days. But how were they supposed to leave if the ferry wasn't running?

We'll have to swim, said Gibraltar in Glennon's mind, but Glennon swiftly pushed that away. Swimming would get them killed.

Today, he'd start figuring out how to leave, but more importantly, he needed to figure out Everett being a vampire.

His handwriting turned into liquid on the page, pencil lead smearing beneath his hand. Painfully, he forced himself to slow down when he wrote about his day for his dad: *Mom bought us matching Moon Boots. She didn't feel well and went to bed early.*

He didn't know what to write about yesterday's creepy events: the way Everett *felt* dangerous, the way he'd grown and shifted and had turned to mist in the reflection of the windows; the way the *Edmund Fitzgerald* had changed shape and grown rust icicles; the way he'd gotten turned around in the woods because of a scary image in the fire; the way the air in the grave-yard had been sad and haunted.

If he wrote a single one of those things down in his letter to his dad, his dad would tell him it was all in his head, just like he did when Glennon woke from nightmares or after he yelled at everyone in the family. *Stop being so dramatic. You're making things up,* Glennon heard his dad say in his head. *You'll be like the boy who cried wolf; no one will ever believe what you have to say if you keep making things up.*

Glennon didn't want that. He didn't want to be told he was too emotional or was exaggerating the situation. He didn't want to be told the scary things on Isle Philippeaux weren't real. He didn't want to be told he was doing a bad job of protecting Mom. He didn't want to be told that he was trying to protect Mom from was something that only existed in his imagination. It all felt too real for it to be fake.

Leaving his room, he slowed, one hand braced against the wall and the other clutching his chest. His heart raced. The pain in his ribs still lingered from last night, though it'd lessened while he'd slept. It was as if the sadness from the graveyard had invaded his body and pierced through to his heart. He shook out his hands, not knowing if he was supposed to tell himself he was imagining the pain or not.

The door to his mom's room creaked open when he pushed it. He peaked in and found Mom sitting in a chair beside her leather suitcase. She undid the clasp and pulled out a jacket over which wide, silver sequins had been sewn.

Glennon pushed the door open farther. "I thought Dad got rid of that jacket. Brought it to Goodwill or something."

She folded the jacket on her lap and petted its soft pink lining. "Oh, he did. I went and got it back."

Dad would be furious if he ever found out Mom had gone behind his back to get the coat. Glennon wouldn't be the one to tell him though.

Light glistened off the silver coins and reflected on her face, drawing Glennon's attention to the dark smudges beneath her eyes. "Are you feeling better? You look tired."

"Why thank you, sweetheart." A small smile tugged at her mouth. "You go have fun with your sister. Don't worry about me. We'll look at schoolwork later. I think I'm going to stay upstairs a bit longer."

Not daring to press his luck, he didn't argue. He had no desire to go through his math books even though they were overdue. He shut the bedroom door, though not before he saw Mom drape the coat over her shoulders. *I don't understand why you have to like dressing up so much,* he remembered his dad saying to her.

Lee sat in the middle of the staircase. She looked at his hand, which still pressed against his chest. "I was worried about you last night. You ran really fast away from the fire."

"Yeah, I didn't like the story," he said, not at all willing to admit he'd seen their dad's face in the flames. If he did, she'd understand why he'd been scared; no part of him wanted to face the sympathetic expression she'd give him. "Is Kit still here?" He'd left Kit on the couch the night before, along with a blanket, a cup of water, and a box of Cheez-Its.

"No," Lee said.

Glennon came down the stairs to check the living room. Sure enough, the cup of water and blanket sat on a table beside the couch, but the box of Cheez-Its was gone. He said, "I wonder where he went."

"I didn't know he stayed here last night."

"He hasn't had any place else to stay, so he's been staying at the keepers' houses still. He's stuck here, like we are." In the kitchen, Glennon poured himself cereal and sat, cradling a spoon in his fist. "What's the plan? We find Everett and what... stick a cross in his face? See if he burns up?"

"An island would be a stupid place for a vampire to live. How would he sneak around and get blood from people without everyone figuring out that something bad was happening?"

"Maybe the entire island is in on it. What if Everett landed here, and now everyone's agreed to supply Everett with blood?"

"We didn't agreed to it! I don't want us to be food for Everett."

A whisper of sound snuck across the wooden floor, and Glennon stopped in the middle of shoving cereal into his mouth. Seamus stuck his head around the entrance to the kitchen, spotted Glennon, hissed, and then backed away.

"He hates me even more now," Glennon mourned.

"What'd you do to him? He came home last night with a dead rat in his mouth. It was so gross. He looked like he'd gotten in a fight too."

"Not a fight, at least not unless he fought with the rat." Glennon pushed his bowl of cereal away, no longer interested in the soggy mess. "I tripped and fell while running. Seamus did not like it."

Frowning, Lee grabbed the back of the jean jacket Glennon wore and pulled him up so he stood. "Come on. We've got research to go do."

"I hate research."

"Only when it's for school and it's on like...how bills become laws or whatever. This sort of research is the good sort."

"Oh?" Glennon twisted out from Lee's grasp. "Is it the sort that has to do with monsters?"

"Yep! It's the sort where we go to Ingram Lighthouse and talk with the biggest storyteller on the isle." Lee seized her own coat from the front closet and zipped it straight up to her throat. "Townsend."

14

Despite the fact that Glennon and Lee had spent the last months biking all over the island, neither of them remembered the road that would take them to Ingram Lighthouse, so they opened the atlas Glennon hadn't yet returned to the First Keeper. He felt bad about it, but considering how poorly made the maps in the atlas were, it didn't seem like the keeper was in dire need of it.

"This looks about as well drawn as if I'd made it." Glennon flipped through the pages. "The roads change on every map."

"It's hand drawn. What do you expect?" Lee said.

"The roads keep *changing*, Lee! They're completely different, and it's just like you said, the lighthouses change too. Graving Lighthouse isn't even on this map." Glennon pointed at one, then tossed the whole atlas onto his bed. "It's more like a piece of modern art than an actual map," he said, not really knowing what modern art looked like. "We'll have to ask Uncle Job."

As it turned out, there was only one main-ish road that

led between Graving and Ingram Lighthouse where Townsend lived. With their Moon Boots on, they biked the five miles across the island to reach the lighthouse. Temperatures had dropped overnight, and the air was crisp and icy when Glennon sucked it into his mouth.

As he biked, the sense of foreboding invaded his senses. Two years ago, he'd gone to a haunted house with Lee and her friends, Cassandra and Lawrence. They'd never been to one before, and Lee was sure she'd love it. Glennon, though, had stepped inside the field where the house had been set up and had immediately known a horrible, terrible thing stood before him, but he hadn't known *why*. The actors inside the haunted house couldn't touch them or hurt them. Surely nothing would go wrong.

Something had gone wrong though; while the actors couldn't touch them, they *could* yell at them. His sister had fallen apart, all the loud, bright pieces of her tucking in until her body was a shell and her personality disappeared somewhere inside. He'd grabbed her hand and pulled her sideways out of the house, figuring Cassandra and Lawrence would be able to find their own way out. Lee had made it outside the haunted house, but not much farther. They'd ended up hiding beneath the back porch, Lee heaving with great, hushed sobs, and him staring into the dark, pretending not to hear.

Glennon didn't quite know why, but as he biked across the isle, the memory of bloodcurdling monster screams and Lee's silent tears and his own shaking fear echoed in his ears.

Townsend's lighthouse came into view. It didn't sit on the edge of a cliff like Graving, but instead rested along a flat shoreline made up of hard rock and a pebbled beach. Red-roofed and white-steepled, the lighthouse resembled a small Catholic church that might be found on the corner of a block in the Twin Cities. The house was one story tall with a small second story rising above where the light sat.

The closer Glennon biked to the pretty image of Ingram Lighthouse before him, the heavier his chest became. A rock sat inside him, weighing down his body. They leaned their bikes against the house and knocked on the back door.

A tall, skinny man with jeans that ended two inches above his ankles and oven mitts on his hands opened the door. Out of the house wafted warmth and the glowing scent of—

"Bread?" Glennon took an involuntary step forward toward the source of the smell.

"Indeed!" said Townsend's dad, Mr. Traxler. He stepped back, asking Glennon and Lee if they wanted to come in with a welcoming motion of his arm.

"We came to see Townsend," Glennon said.

"You didn't come for my bread?" Mr. Traxler joked.

"I did!" Glennon said, and Mr. Traxler laughed.

Glennon smiled at the laugh, though he watched Mr. Traxler closely. He knew how fast a laugh could switch into something else, something made of roaring anger and broken things. He noticed Lee watching Mr. Traxler too, and so he nodded at her to go first, putting his body between her and Mr. Traxler when they entered the house.

The livable space in Ingram was much smaller than the keepers' houses at Graving. Glennon saw two bedrooms, a kitchen, a living room with a fireplace, and a bathroom. Other than that, there wasn't much too it. A metal staircase wound straight through the center of the living room and to the light on the second floor.

In the kitchen, they found Townsend sitting at the table beside Keeper Delmont—Ingram's lighthouse keeper—eating a piece of steaming, soft white bread. Townsend paused with a slice halfway to her mouth.

"We need to ask you a question," Glennon said to her.

She set down her bread. "Are you sure you didn't come here to yell at me about the ghost story?"

"I never yell at people," Glennon said, sickened at the thought. He never wanted to become a person who yelled.

Townsend folded her arms, tightening the black coat she never seemed to take off. She turned to her dad and said, "I scared Glennon with a story so bad that he fell off the log he was sitting on and then ran into the woods."

"You didn't scare me!" Glennon said.

Mr. Traxler set his oven mitts on the table and asked, "You were telling ghost stories again?"

Townsend hesitated, then said, "Yeah. Sorry."

Mr. Traxler shook his head and smiled sadly at Glennon. "She's scared me a time or two with her stories as well."

Glennon found himself eying Mr. Traxler and Townsend, at the gentle way her dad handed her another piece of bread and scolded her for making her stories so scary. Townsend had a wild imagination too, but her dad didn't make her feel bad about it. He wondered what that was like.

Townsend pushed up from the table. "We can talk upstairs where these two won't eavesdrop." My dads are nosey. She pointed her thumb at her dad and the keeper.

They headed up the metal staircase to the second floor, where they found themselves in a very small room. At the center stood a massive glossy light. Panels of glass layered one on top of the other to form the intricate bulb.

Large windows took the place of the opposite wall and revealed Superior before them. The waters outside were dark, nearly black-blue, and a chalky film of clouds covered over the sky.

"What question do you have?" Townsend asked.

Glennon readied the words *Does a vampire live on Isle Philippeaux?* but before he could ask, he noticed someone moving along the beach, heading away from the lighthouse.

"Who's that?" Glennon jabbed his finger against the window.

Townsend didn't bother looking where he pointed. "It's probably Gibraltar."

"The sailor? I saw him in the shipyard yesterday." The man had run away from Everett.

"He's been walking the beach all day, collecting sea glass. My dad found him trying to swim off the island last night." A deep frown crossed Townsend's face. "He was paddling around in the cold."

Glennon's heart fell. For some reason, it felt like it was his fault Gibraltar had tried to swim off Isle Philippeaux. "That's... Why would he do that?"

"He said staying on Isle Philippeaux was worse than drowning."

"Why? What's so bad about this place—" Glennon cut himself off. "It's because of the vampire, isn't it?"

"*What*," Townsend said, voice flat.

"See..." Glennon tried to explain, but old nervousness flared up in him. He felt stupid now, trying to talk through the idea that Everett might be a vampire.

"Glennon saw Everett being creepy the other day," Lee said.

"Lots of people are creepy. It doesn't make them vampires," Townsend said.

Lee held up a finger. "True, but Everett doesn't have a reflection, and we've never seen him in the sun, *and* we think he did something to our mom. She's been extremely tired and acting not-herself ever since she met him."

Townsend pulled up her hood from where it'd been laying across her back. "Those are good clues, but...no, Everett isn't a vampire. Besides, why would a vampire live on a small island when he could go literally anywhere else?"

"We wondered that," Lee said. "We thought maybe the whole isle had made some weird pact with him. Maybe people supply him with blood, and he protects them in exchange."

A loud laugh exploded out of Townsend. "A pact. Right, okay... Like I said, though, Everett isn't a vampire."

If Everett wasn't a vampire, then what was he? A werewolf? Did werewolves have reflections? Right now, Glennon couldn't even think of other sorts of monsters that existed.

The niggling sense that something was going sideways filled him. He'd spent his whole life being spun in circles when talking with his dad. He knew what it sounded like when someone was *not* answering a question directly. He dug through how Townsend had responded, and said, "Everett isn't a vampire, but...has the isle made some sort of pact with him?"

Townsend's eyes sparked, widening the slightest. "As far as I know, the people on the island haven't made any sort of specific pact with Everett."

Lee said, "As far as you know?"

Townsend said, "Yeah. As far as I know."

Glennon turned back to the window and set his elbows on the sill. *As far as she knows.* What was it then that Townsend didn't know? He felt like she was hinting at something, he just didn't know what. Why wouldn't she just come out and say the truth?

Far above, the clouds thinned, letting sunlight loose from the sky. He blinked and squinted out the window. What he'd assumed was a tall rock jutting out of Superior in the distance turned out to be...another lighthouse?

"How many lighthouses does Isle Philippeaux have?" Glennon asked, thinking of the First Keeper's strange atlas that had dozens of pictures of the same island, all of them slightly different.

She said, "It depends."

"On what?" Lee asked.

Her expression turned cold. A muscle in her cheek twitched. "On electricity and supplies. Sometimes we don't have all the energy we need to operate all the lighthouses."

"That sounds dangerous," Glennon said.

"It can be. Yes."

Air puffed through the molding that surrounded the huge window before them. It chilled Glennon, and he pulled his jacket tighter around him even as he turned away from Lee and faced the new lighthouse. "That lighthouse looks like it's floating on water."

Townsend said, "It's a crib lighthouse, called Spectre Lighthouse. It's built on concrete right on the shoals. It makes it look like it's floating. A keeper lives there, but they refuse to turn on the light. It doesn't matter, though, because our lighthouse is located so close to it." Townsend tugged on her hood, pulling it over her face, even more. "You can't go there."

Glennon heard a small snap in her voice, a hint of the harsh *don't ask about it again* tone his dad often used.

Townsend headed down the stairs, and Lee followed, but Glennon paused, staying in the room a moment longer. He watched out the window, and as he did, the smallest gleam of light appeared in the uppermost tower of Spectre Lighthouse. He swore someone stood in that window and waved at him, beckoned him to come visit.

The thing inside Glennon that had filled with foreboding while biking to Ingram fell open, stretching wide. They'd come to Townsend for answers, but she'd told them nothing. In fact, she'd danced away from answers. And right now, he stared at a place that held exactly the answers he needed. He knew it.

He just had to cross Superior to get there.

15

Spectre Lighthouse hovered atop the water in the distance.
Glennon stood on the beach that surrounded Ingram. A little
to his right, Townsend's boat bobbed in the lake.

"What are you doing?" Lee called to him. She stood over
her bike, one foot propped on a pedal.

"I want to go see that lighthouse," Glennon said.

"Why?"

"Because Townsend didn't want us to go there."

"So? It's not like Everett lives there."

"I know, but…" A complicated set of emotions swelled in
Glennon—confusion and anger and curiosity and fear.

"Glennon?" Lee asked.

He didn't know how to explain anything he felt, and that
made his words shrink too small for him to find. He couldn't
talk. He could hardly think.

"Earth to Glennon?"

Cat got your tongue? Have nothing to say? In her voice,
Glennon heard his dad's.

"Why do you want to go there?" Lee asked again.

Speak! You stupid child. How are you mine—

"I'm going home." Lee twisted her hands on her bike handles, almost like she was revving the engine of a motorcycle. "I'm going to see if Mom'll let me make a long-distance call. I wanna try and call Cassandra to ask her about monsters. Maybe she'll know something else that Everett could be."

Glennon swallowed hard and found some words. "Maybe ask her about werewolves."

"Are you going to stay here for a bit?"

He nodded and turned back to the lighthouse, not watching Lee bike away from him. He focused on Spectre Lighthouse while trying to smoosh away the panic he always felt when he couldn't figure out what to say.

The cement-gray lighthouse rose out of the water. Four square windows stacked vertically along its height, and wide rectangular windows encircled the uppermost level. Its pointed top was painted red and had a ball at its tip, almost as if the lighthouse wore a red beanie with a small yarn poof.

He didn't know how to get to the lighthouse. If Kit were there, he'd probably help; he'd be brave enough to borrow Townsend's boat...*and* he probably knew how to actually work the motor.

Crunching rattles came from behind Glennon. He turned,

expecting to see Lee, but instead, the beach stood empty—just Ingram and piles of rocks and a few skinny trees. A light breeze washed over the shore. A rainbow pinwheel beside Ingram spun in silent circles. Nothing else stood before him, except as he waited, two eyes peered up and over a boulder—*a rat.*

A rat just like Everett's rat. Like the one on his mom's windowsill. Like the one that had tried to climb the couch to attack her like the ones that had destroyed the engine of the ferry.

It lifted itself up on its hind legs, nibbling on something it held between its paws. The squeak of its teeth biting through the food made Glennon recoil. A pebble to Glennon's right tumbled, and the slight sound of it rang out. He jerked toward it, and he found a second rat staring at him. A third crept past the second, its claws scraping against stone as it scurried closer. Its skull pushed against the fur of its face, and awkward angles formed around its eyes. Sharp teeth glinted in its wide-open mouth.

Nerves on high alert, he spun and rushed to Townsend's boat, trying to get away. He shoved at it, digging his toes into the fist-sized rocks. It gave an inch, then a foot. He undid the tie to the metal pole, pushed again, and then hopped in when it bobbed free on the water.

Gripping the edge of the boat, Glennon held on, trying not

to get his shoes wet. He jumped and flopped headfirst into the boat, then rolled his legs in as well. On the back of Townsend's boat was the motor, though it was tilted so the blades stayed out of the water and off the rocks. A pair of oars lay on the hull. They were unwieldy hunks of wood, and he struggled to lift one up and over the edge of the boat to shove at the rocks.

"What are you doing?"

Glennon twisted. Townsend stood on the beach, hood pulled low over her brow and arms folded across her chest. Only her hands showed from beneath her coat, her white skin shading blue in the wintry light of day. He glanced behind her, eyes wide and breath coming in short gasps, in the way it often did when he was afraid. The rats were gone.

"You're stealing my boat," she said.

"Uhh." Glennon shoved at the rocks with the oar again. "Borrowing. I'm borrowing it."

"Do you even know how to work a boat?"

He glanced at the motor he didn't know how to lower and the oars he didn't know how to paddle.

"You're trying to go to Spectre Lighthouse, aren't you?"

Glennon felt the lighthouse behind him, felt the light he'd seen in the uppermost window blinking at the back of his head. It tapped on his skull. It said, *I know the answers to your questions.*

"I told you not to go there." Townsend's voice darkened.

He plunged the oar into the water again. It skidded against the stones.

Townsend's head tipped. The smallest flicker of tawny rope fiber fell out from under her hood, hanging down like the tips of hair. "You're *stealing my boat*, and you're doing it to go somewhere I *told you not to go*."

Townsend's voice turned angry and cruel, and in response, Glennon's body changed stance. He lowered into the boat and braced his feet against the sides. He watched her, trying to guess what her anger would make her do.

"Get *out* of my *boat*!"

But Glennon wouldn't get out. He didn't have a choice. He had to get to Spectre Lighthouse; if he didn't, he might not find out what was happening with Mom. He said, "No," and heard his voice tremble.

"GET OUT!" Townsend shook with anger.

"My mom's getting the life sucked out of her by a monster! I'm going to that lighthouse, and you can't stop me!" Glennon said, not quite able to make himself yell as loud as Townsend did.

Townsend slowly dropped her arms to her sides. Her hands came out farther from under her sleeves and, for a moment, swollen and puffy skin became visible, almost like bread dough set out to rise too long. She leapt forward, setting one hand on the edge of the boat and lofting herself straight into the hull. She landed with both feet flat, her gross hands hidden back under her sleeves.

Glennon backed away from her. He scrabbled across the hull, running into a tackle box and the other oar and then the front seat.

"I don't like thieves," Townsend said, her voice not at all sounding like her voice. It was low and terrible, and it sickened Glennon because he'd grown up listening to a voice just like that.

He knew how quickly an angry voice could turn into angry actions. He knew how quickly anger could turn a person into someone entirely new. He didn't want to watch Townsend transform into something cruel in the same way his dad did when angry.

Townsend bent toward him. "And I don't like people who don't listen to me when I give them good advice."

The knobs of Glennon's spine pressed to the seat behind him. It reminded him of the benches in the canoe his dad had once taken him in.

Why aren't you having fun? his dad had asked on that trip. The paddle in Glennon's hands had felt strange and the muscles in his chest had ached and the hot sun had made his head hurt. When he'd looked at the water moving swiftly next to the canoe, he'd thought of drowning. *You're supposed to have fun. I took you on this trip so you could have fun. HAVE FUN!*

Glennon thoughts spun out of control. The past overlapped with now. He pushed at the clear memory, trying to shove it down into himself, into the place he stored things so that he wouldn't have to look at them straight. This moment was not *that* moment, and he hated his brain for making him think it was the same. It wasn't the same. *It wasn't!*

"I'm sorry," Glennon whispered. He had no other words. He held up his hands, as if trying to ward her off or protect his body from her anger. "I'm sorry."

Townsend turned her hooded form from him. She didn't respond. Glennon watched her longer, knowing he could stay in this moment of watchfulness for as long as he needed. He would stand still until he knew he was safe and could move.

"I'm sorry too," Townsend said.

What? Glennon's brain didn't quite process what she'd said. Townsend was sorry? But…he'd never had someone apologize to *him* before; it didn't make sense.

"My emotions got the best of me." Townsend rubbed her forehead with the back of one wrist that was cocooned inside her jacket. "I shouldn't have yelled."

"No, you shouldn't have," Glennon said beneath his breath, but then quickly zipped shut his mouth. He'd never said out loud before that he should've been treated better when someone was mad. What had made him do that now?

Townsend sat down hard on the back bench. "If you really want to go to the lighthouse, I'll take you. But I'll warn you, the going will be rough."

"I want to go." Glennon's arms shook while he levered himself up and onto the front seat. He felt wobbly inside, though he tried not to let Townsend see it. "The weather's calm, and it's not too far."

"It's farther than it looks, and the weather here tends to change without notice." Townsend unhooked something at the back of the boat, and he heard the motor dip into the water. It started up with a hushed growl. "When this is all over, don't say that I didn't warn you. Hold tight please."

The boat gave a little kick, and Glennon had to adjust how he sat so he wouldn't fall over. Wind whooshed against his face, reminding of the day they'd ridden the ferry from Minnesota to Isle Philippeaux. That day had been bright and warm, the sort of day that felt like winter but looked like spring. Out of nowhere, Isle Philippeaux had flickered into existence on the horizon, a dark blob of land marring Superior's glittering water.

Glennon glanced around as they flew toward Spectre Lighthouse. A shadow hovered at the edge of his vision. It took on the blurred outline of a person, arms stretching long and reaching out to grab him. When he looked straight at the shape, he saw that nothing rode atop the waves. He scanned the water, and the shadow at the periphery of his vision appeared again, a dark blotch that grabbed at the edges of his clothes. He shrank into himself, no longer thinking of bright, warm days.

"Hold tight." Townsend's voice had changed again, though this time, it didn't hold anger. It held *fear*. Storm clouds spun across the sky, swallowing up whatever sun had shone through before.

Behind them, only the thinnest of gray clouds hovered above Ingram Lighthouse. Not one black cloud sunk its talons over the isle; they all stayed directly over his head. His hands crept out and gripped the edge of his seat, fingers turning into metal hooks, moving almost without permission to hold him fast.

16

Lake Superior wallowed in herself. She yawned open, all maw with foaming spittle and lapping tongues. Into the bottom of one cavernous wave, Townsend's boat descended.

Glennon screamed. It ripped from his throat and he didn't think twice about it. This was *not* the sort of fear he was used to.

"HOLD ON," Townsend screamed over the sound of the wind that encircled him.

Glennon tried to say, *I am holding on!* but all that came out was "*AHHHH!!*" as they shot over one wave and thumped onto another.

The lake chomped down on them. Wood screeched—he hadn't known wood could make noise like that—as the lake and its many-hundred jaws scraped against the bottom. When they came to the top of one massive tongue of water, he swore he saw a flash of light that lit up the lighthouse, revealing the figure of a person—its keeper.

The boat poured down the other side of the wave, taking

them with it, and at the bottom, Glennon screamed again, because the shadowed figure he'd seen at the edge of his vision stood in the trough. It was lit entirely from within by a bright, glowing light. It burned Glennon's eyes and made him see spots. In one hand, it held a rope that formed a lasso on one end and whipped it toward Glennon.

Zoom! Townsend kicked up the boat's motor, flying them out of reach of the shadow. They went up another wave and down again, and when they crashed to the bottom, the shadow and its rope was there, flinging it over Glennon's shoulders.

The rope looped around Glennon's chest, and as he stared down at it, he saw it was made of smoke. It was thin and translucent and looked like it shouldn't exist, and yet, as it tightened around his body, it *hurt*. It tugged him toward the shadow.

"Don't let go!" Townsend screamed.

Glennon shoved his feet against the side of the boat, refusing to let the creature pull him over the edge and into Superior.

"Just a little farther." Townsend's voice held Glennon fast.

"I won't go!" Glennon yelled at the creature. He had to get to the lighthouse. He needed answers, and he needed to help Mom! "You can't make me! Not *now*!"

Townsend angled the boat over a wave. They fell over its lip, and suddenly, the frenzy of the lake stopped.

The abrupt release of the storm and the absence of the

smokey rope around his chest left him woozy. He leaned forward and toppled off his seat, just as the boat itself rubbed along the shoals. They bumped into the cemented side of the lighthouse.

Shivers wracked his body. His clothes were soaked through. His waterlogged skin froze, and not even the trembling of his muscles could warm him. He hadn't known how cold he was during the storm—too much of him had been wrapped tight in fear to understand he was turning hypothermic.

"Glad to see you made it," said a voice from above them, and Glennon looked up to see Spectre Lighthouse's keeper. He stood on the cement foundation, hands set on his hips and arms akimbo. He nodded at Townsend, saying, "Good to see you again, Ms. Traxler. I see you brought me a visitor."

Townsend waved. She didn't shiver like Glennon, and she wasn't wet like him either. How had she managed to stay dry on their trip? "I won't be coming in today. Glennon's the one who's come to see you."

Glennon sat upright, feeling sick. "I'm Glennon."

The keeper, his head shaded by a flat-brimmed hat, came to the metal ladder that crawled over the edge of the cement foundation and into the water. He held out a hand, and Glennon reached to take it, but his fingers slid straight through his palm. He jerked back and stared hard at his numb hand that was covered with water. What a mean trick for his mind to play.

"*Ahh*, sorry." The keeper wiped his hand on the rough cloth of their pants and held it out again. This time, when Glennon grabbed for it, he held fast and pulled him up the ladder.

The lighthouse was exactly as small as it'd looked from the distance. A tall, cylindrical tower shot up from the center, and a wide cement walkway wrapped around it. Glennon peered over the edge of the foundation to see the lake just two feet below. Through the clear liquid, he spotted rock and pebbles, turned smooth by the water.

He turned back to the keeper and through his chattering teeth said, "You're a woman!" though he promptly blushed furiously and clamped his mouth together. If Lee were here, she would've punched him in the arm, and if Mom were here, she would've glared at him in a way that would've shriveled his heart, and really...he felt horrible. Why had he assumed the keeper was a man?

The keeper said, "And you're going to die of the cold if we don't get you inside to warm up."

Glennon glanced at Townsend, not understanding why she didn't join them. Didn't she need to warm up too?

Glennon followed the keeper inside the small house where

she gestured for him to sit in front of a heating element that had been placed dead center of the living space. The keeper handed him dry clothes and a wool blanket, then disappeared to a side room and waited for Glennon to change.

He pulled on the clothes, feeling as if he'd been transported to the 1800s, with suspenders and itchy pants and hand-knitted socks that pulled up to his knees.

When the keeper returned, she hung each of his clothes to dry. They sizzled, steam rising from the cloth. She said, "It is surprisingly easy to die from hypothermia. You need warm clothes on your outsides and something warm on your insides. Both parts of you are equally important."

Glennon tucked the blanket around his shoulders. He accepted the mug of tea she handed him, and even though he didn't actually like drinking tea, he sucked it down. Warmth slid into his throat and heated his stomach, easing the shivers that clenched tight his muscles.

"I didn't know women could be Keepers," Glennon admitted, feeling the shame of the assumption deep inside his chest.

"The only times women are limited in what they can be, it's because someone else has told them they cannot be something." The keeper bent a little, meeting Glennon's gaze. "Are you telling me I cannot be something?"

"N-no." Glennon shook his head hard.

"Good. You would be surprised to know how many women have been keepers of lighthouses throughout history." She straightened. Her voice held a whisper of an accent that Glennon found calming. "I am Keeper Sanz. My husband and I came here from Spain. He was to be Keeper at a lighthouse in Duluth, but he died."

"Oh," Glennon said.

"People die." She lifted one shoulder. "This is how I ended up as Keeper here, and now, why are you here? There are only two reasons people ever visit me: they want answers or they want me turn on the light. Which is it?"

"I came for answers," Glennon said.

Keeper Sanz stared at him, and he stared back, and slowly he realized she was waiting for him to ask a question.

"I…" Glennon stumbled beneath all of the questions he had. They ran through his head, and he picked out the least risky of them to begin with: "Why don't you turn on the light?"

"The light benefits the isle, and I've no wish to help it."

"But…lighthouses keep ships from crashing."

"Do they?" Keeper Sanz raised her eyebrows.

"Yes." The whole point of lighthouses was to keep ships from wrecking. "If the isle wants the light turned on so bad, why don't they hire a new keeper?"

Keeper Sanz smiled, her teeth making Glennon feel as if

he stared at small pearly fangs. "They've tried, but I've been here a *long* time. It's not so easy to move a person who's tied to a place as some would like to think. I'm too good at haunting this place." She tapped her fingers against the seat of her chair. "Now, what's the real question you've come to ask me?"

Glennon sorted through what he knew and realized how little he *did* know. He settled on the one solid question he and Lee had come up with: "There's a sailor I—Everett. I think he might be a vampire. He's done something to hurt my mom."

"I've met Everett," she said. "Asking if Everett is a vampire isn't your real question."

"But it *is*."

The keeper cocked her head to the side. Something seemed to recalculate inside her mind. "Everett is not a vampire."

He clenched both hands around the mug. Then he asked the real question he needed an answer to: "How do I help my mom?"

Keeper Sanz's eyes softened at the edges. "I don't know your mother, but I should think it isn't your responsibility to help; you're a child. It's your mother's job to help *you*."

Except...he needed to help Mom. He had to. That *was* his job!

"The questions you're looking for answers to aren't as concrete as you think," Keeper Sanz said. "Questions like: How can we be haunted both by the past and by the future? How can a thing that is dead still be alive? How long can we lie to ourselves about terrible truths before they destroy us?"

He curled tight into himself, confused.

"Those are your questions." Keeper Sanz leaned forward. Amber light from an overhead lamp shadowed her features and turned her hair into the silk nests that webworms spun over trees. "Glennon, how long have you been lying to yourself?"

He stood. "I don't lie to myself!"

"If you're saying that, you're lying even worse than I imagined." Abruptly, Keeper Sanz stood as well. She turned away from Glennon and began to rummage through the drawers of a table pressed beneath one window. Glennon backed away and toward the door. Before he could exit and escape to Townsend, he caught sight of newspaper clippings that covered the windows. He read the faded writing. *SS Western Reserve* 1892, *The Hudson* 1901, *SS Bannockburn* 1902, *Leafield* 1913, *Henry B. Smith* 1913, *SS Kamloops* 1927, *SS Edmund Fitzgerald* 1975, *USCGC Mesquite* December 4, 1989.

Every single crisp, crinkled article reported the tale of a shipwreck or a disappeared ship or the deaths of sailors.

Except...one ship's name caught his eye. The *Mesquite*. Sunk on December 4, 1989. The *Mesquite* had been the coast guard ship that had helped the *Anabeth*, and December 4, 1989 was weeks ago.

Glennon didn't understand, and not understanding made him want to run away. He always ran or froze, and he hated it, but he didn't know what else to do. He reached out and gripped the door handle, then asked aloud, "What am I supposed to *do*?"

"You find the truth of what haunts you," Keeper Sanz said from behind him.

"But I'm not haunted." He turned and found her holding out a small gold compact in the shape of an oval. In her opposite hand, she held a bag with his still-wet clothing. She shoved both at him, and he took them, if only to stop her approach. A small latch held the compact closed. When he undid it, it popped open like a clamshell, and he found himself staring at two mirrors, each showing his reflection. He went to face it toward the keeper, but she closed her hand over it.

"Mirrors do a lovely job of showing us the truth of things." She pressed his fingers and snapped the compact mirror shut.

Glennon clasped it to his side. Mom had read Grimm's Fairy Tales to them when they were young. He knew about the magic mirror in Snow White. He hesitated, then asked, "Is this magic?"

"Magic isn't real."

"But—"

"The mirror will show you the true form of Isle Philippeaux. That's all you need to know." Keeper Sanz pursed her lips, locking away her secrets. She reached past him to the door and swung it open. When Glennon exited, he looked back and found she didn't stand in the doorway. Perhaps she'd headed up toward the top of the lighthouse to watch as they sailed away.

Glennon climbed down the ladder and into the boat. The skies above them were dark, though they were only dark in the way that a disappearing sun on the horizon darkened the day, not a storm.

He dropped onto his seat. Frustrated, he said, "That was the most pointless conversation I've ever had. I didn't get any of the answers I needed. Instead, she just listed questions to me. She accused me of lying."

"Keeper Sanz isn't always the most helpful." Townsend started the motor, and they started puttering across the lake.

Glennon opened the mirror, using it to look over his shoulder at the receding lighthouse behind them, wanting to catch a glimpse of Keeper Sanz.

In the mirror, though, he didn't see the lighthouse or the keeper, he saw *Townsend*...except he didn't see Townsend, he saw a thing of blustering wind and twisting smoke and eyes that were thick with fog, and strands of frayed rope that whipped out from under her black, tattered hood. Her arms were made of the oars of a boat.

Townsend looked straight at him, her filmy eyes hard inside her hazy skull, and in a voice made of the flood of water against eardrums said, "You shouldn't have done that."

17

Glennon flung himself to the opposite side of the boat, nearly tipping over its edge in his hurry to get away from the thing behind him. A deep well of sadness filled the air above the boat, rising like a tide. His fear of the creature collided with the depthless sorrow, and tears pricked at his eyes. This was exactly what he'd felt when he'd stood in the graveyard with Kit!

Whatever monster it was that he'd thought lived on the island wasn't on the island. It was in the boat with him.

He pressed his spine to the bow, trying to get a good look at the thing that sat behind him, except when he looked, he didn't see the creature with its body made of smoke and water and doughy skin. He saw…"Townsend?"

"What." She sat straight, her smooth black coat hiding her expression.

"You—" His heart whomped inside his chest. He pointed at her, then at the mirror. "You were…"

He held up the compact. Towensend's image shifted at

once, the reflection showing slivers of wood embedded in her stormy body. A metal fishing hook stuck through one thigh. The clacking pebbles of deep waters rattled in her chest, visible through the coat that had become little more than a sheer, tattered piece of fabric. Her face caught his attention, horror magnifying the way her cheeks were made of soppy, sodden, wrinkly skin.

Mirrors do a lovely job of showing us the truth of things, Keeper Sanz had said. But how was this the truth of things? What *was* Townsend? What sort of creature looked like it was made of items that had sunk to Superior's depths?

His gaze dragged up to her face, where that same skin encircled her eyes. It was drowned skin, dead skin. Skin that would slough off and reveal bone if he were to brush up against her.

He'd seen that face before, though it'd been for only a split second when he'd stood on the beach of Graving Bay with Townsend and Kit. He'd sworn his mind was playing tricks on him, then.

Do you believe what you saw? Lee had asked him. He hadn't believed, but he should have.

"What *are* you?" he asked.

Townsend's voice creaked, the same aching moans her boat had made during the storm. "What do you think I am?"

"I..." He needed Lee. He needed someone who was smarter than him. He needed—"You look just like the thing that followed us during the storm! I thought I made that up!"

"You didn't."

"What *was* it? What are you? You're a..." He didn't know what to call her—a creature? A thing? A...*monster*? He said again, "What are you?"

Her eyes gleamed, both terrible and beautiful at once. "If you don't know, I'm not about to tell you."

He snapped shut the mirror in anger. Why did she refuse to tell him *anything*? Why didn't anyone on this island tell the truth?

Glennon faced Townsend the rest of the ride. There was no way he was going to risk putting his back to her.

"Two days," Glennon murmured to himself. He just had to make it two more days, then they'd be gone. No more mysteries. No more magic. No more *monsters*. He'd find a way to get off the isle by then, even if it meant taking Townsend's tiny boat all the way across Lake Superior.

"Two days until The Waning," Townsend said.

"Two days until we leave."

"Two days until everyone leaves."

What did *that* mean? He felt as if she wanted him to ask about The Waning, as if she knew he had no clue what the celebration was for. He refused to rise to the bait. Instead he said, "I don't care what The Waning is."

"You should." Her voice darkened, creaking in the same way it had when she'd transformed in the mirror. It left an awful, hollow pit inside his stomach.

Quiet, he asked, "What's The Waning, Townsend?"

Her chin dropped. Her hood fell farther over her brow. She said, "If you don't know, I'm not about to tell you."

———

Thoughts of monsters spun through Glennon's head as he headed back to Graving. He biked as if Townsend chased him, as if something with clawed hands hovered over his shoulder, as if the island's creepy rats were following behind.

He was a mess of questions, of confusions, of memories that made no sense: the creature in the water trying to toss a lasso over his shoulders; Townsend transforming in the reflection of the mirror, showing her true form; his dad saying, *A lake cannot "like" to sink ships, Lee.*

What was Townsend? It seemed that all of his questions could be answered if he just knew what sort of creature Townsend was. Was Townsend the same thing that Everett was? Was he supposed to be scared of Townsend in the same way he was scared of Everett?

He needed Lee—why couldn't he be smarter? Why couldn't he remember things better or put together puzzles? He'd always been terrible at the word puzzles their dad sometimes told at dinner. This felt like one of those moments, sitting at the supper table, with his dad staring hard at him, saying, *Think. If you think and look at all your clues, you'll come up with the right answer. Your brain has holes in it, doesn't it, Glen? Why aren't you thinking? Think!*

Thoughts consumed him, so much so that when he finally remembered to pay attention to his surroundings, he didn't recognize a single twist in the road. He let the bike coast and stuck out his foot when he slowed too much to balance. Nothing looked familiar. A deep valley covered in browning moss cut away to his right. To his left, a pine forest that was devoid of actual pine needles covered the landscape. Surely he would remember biking past sickly trees that all looked like Charlie Brown's Christmas tree.

"There's only one road," he said to himself, trying to be rational. He cleared his throat and tried to talk as calmly as Uncle Job had that morning when giving them directions. "There's only one road between Graving and Ingram. You can't get lost if you stay on it."

A squeak and a chirp sounded behind him. Adrenaline shot through him as the memory of rats rose in his mind. He didn't dare turn around to look and instead started biking as fast as he could.

The ride back to Graving took twice as long as the ride to Ingram, and he never managed to come up with any answers to his questions. When he finally made it, it was early evening. Graving's beam of light shot out over the lake. He shoved his bike into the shed and bolted for the Third Keeper's house, where Uncle Job pushed an empty wheelbarrow across the front lawn.

Think, he told himself. *Think!*

"I'm not smart enough, Uncle Job!" Glennon shouted, surprising both himself and his uncle.

Uncle Job set down the wheelbarrow and faced him, giving Glennon all his attention. He asked, "Who told you that you aren't smart?"

Glennon's mouth opened, but no words hovered inside. Why was *that* the question Uncle Job asked? Wasn't it obvious he wasn't smart?

"My dad used to tell me that I wasn't smart. It wasn't true though. I grew up and learned that there are a hundred different sorts of smart. You are your own sort of smart, but don't doubt that you *are* smart." Uncle Job said this as he said everything else, with quiet certainty. It disturbed something inside of Glennon, as if some piece of the foundation inside himself had shifted over an inch. The disturbing *hurt*.

"Oh," Glennon said.

Uncle Job picked back up the handles to his wheelbarrow. "People will tell you terrible things all your life, Glennon. Some of those things will live and grow inside you, but them living and growing inside you doesn't mean they're true." He continued pushing the barrow toward one of the small sheds that kept supplies for the lighthouse, leaving Glennon alone beside the door.

All of Glennon's swirling thoughts ground to a halt. He focused on the low reverberations of Uncle Job's voice. *You are your own sort of smart.*

What sort of smart was he, if Uncle Job was right?

All of his tired muscles relaxed. He'd told himself so many times in past days that he wasn't smart and that he couldn't remember things. What if he'd been wrong every time he'd said that?

His mind crawled back to the last time he'd remembered saying those words to himself. Keeper Sanz's hand had slid right through his, and he'd thought it'd been a mean trick his mind had played on him. What if it hadn't been a mean trick at all? What if his brain had been paying attention to exactly what it needed to pay attention to?

What sorts of creatures didn't have reflections *and* were invisible *and* didn't have mass *and* had different forms they could take on?

Inside the house, Seamus lounged on the first step of the stairs. Peeling one eye open, he didn't so much as twitch a muscle when Glennon stepped over him and headed to the bedroom he shared with Lee.

He flung open the door and found his sister buried in a book.

Lee slammed the book shut and yelled, "Where have you *been*?" at the same time he yelled, "I know what they are!"

They both stared at one another, not knowing who should speak first.

He leaned back out of the threshold to the door and peered down the hall. "Where's Mom?" he asked, instead of answering her question or repeating his.

Lee folded her arms, the book tucked against her chest. "She's still in bed. She looks awful. *Where have you been?* We went biking to Townsend's this morning, and you've been gone for hours and hours. It's almost dinner."

"The bike ride home took a really long time," Glennon said.

"What'd you do? Stop and smell roses?"

"No, I..." Glennon stopped, not knowing how to explain the events from the day. His words froze inside him.

Lee set her book down on the floor and leaned forward. "Tell me," she said in a steady voice that reminded Glennon of Uncle Job.

Relief turned Glennon's knees to jelly. He closed the door and flopped onto the floor, his back pressed against the wall. Lee had never, not once that he could remember in his entire life, doubted him. Not even now.

Strange, magical things don't happen in real life, whispered their dad inside his head, but he opened his mouth and started talking to Lee, drowning out their dad's voice. He told her every piece of the day he could remember, even the pieces he couldn't *exactly* remember, like the storm and the creature in the water. Details in those moments turned fuzzy and desperate, skewing inside his mind in the same way that memories of his dad often did.

"You were scared," Lee said, when he complained that he couldn't remember enough. "Sometimes when I'm scared, I can't remember anything, but other times, I remember everything."

By the time he finished, Glennon found he was very tired. Telling the truth was, apparently, exhausting. He let himself pause and breathe, and realized that talking about the scary, confusing things helped settle his thoughts. About the ghost story Townsend had told the other night and the image that had appeared in the fire. About the way his hand had slid through Keeper Sanz's hand and the dead-looking rats that kept appearing. About the road back to Graving, how it had been unending and how he'd traveled past terrain he'd never seen before. And, too, about the entire, haunted feel of Isle Philippeaux.

"I think they're ghosts," Glennon said at last.

Before, when he'd said out loud that Everett might be a vampire, he hadn't believed it. Not really. And it hadn't made much sense when he'd considered werewolves. But when the word *ghosts* rolled out of his mouth, something about it felt right and true. Tension left his body, muscles that had been wound tight since the storm and the boat ride with Townsend unlocked, leaving him tired...but also pleased. He'd figured it out.

"Everett's a ghost?" Lee murmured. "That makes sense. Ghosts are usually tied to something. They haunt places or people."

"They've got to be haunting Isle Philippeaux, but who are they haunting? *Us?* Are they haunting us?"

"I have no idea. How are you supposed to tell if you're being haunted?"

"Is that what's wrong with Mom? Is she being haunted?"

Lee looked up at him, mouth flattened into a thin line. She asked the question then that had already started to gnaw at Glennon. "If she's being haunted, how do we stop it?"

18

"You like macaroni and cheese, right?" Uncle Job shifted a little in the kitchen, though he didn't quite turn to face them.

Glennon and Lee stood in the doorway between the kitchen and dining room. They knew Uncle Job usually cooked for himself, but since they'd arrived, Mom had done most of the cooking for them. Tonight, though, they found him and not Mom stirring a wooden spoon in a pot filled with beans. A second pot held yellow, cheesy noodles.

Uncle Job pointed with his opposite hand to the table in the dining room. "The mail arrived. Looks like you have something from your dad, Glennon."

Glennon's heart kicked up, and for the first time in days, it wasn't because of fear. He skittered out of the kitchen and into the dining room. There, he found an envelope addressed to *Glen McCue* in his dad's looping script, a big wave curling up from the *n* at the end to encircle the rest of his name from above.

"It's not a postcard," he said to Lee, hand trembling a little as he grabbed it up. "It's a whole letter!"

"He never sends actual letters." She peered over his shoulder.

Glennon tore into it. Mail took weeks to get from Minnesota to Brussels where his dad was teaching. That meant this had to be his dad's response from one of the first letters Glennon sent from Isle Philippeaux. Pinching the folded paper inside the envelope, he slid out the letter, noticing the small blue lines that crossed the paper. It looked exactly like the blue lines in the composition notebook Glennon wrote in. His dad must write in the same sort of notebook he did. He really had no idea what his dad's life was like when he went overseas to teach. This made him feel like maybe he knew *something* though; they wrote in the same notebook!

He shook out the folded papers and held them so the light in the dining room shone over his dad's curling writing.

Today, we stepped onto Isle Philippeaux, and every~ thing inside me felt sick.

Cold washed through Glennon's body, and he dropped the paper. The sheafs fluttered down, their folds rustling as they descended. They fell to the floor and stared up at him. It was *his* chicken scratch that ran on top of the blue lines, not his dad's script. And through the scrawls of Glennon's own writing ran harsh lines made in permanent, red ink.

Tentatively, he crouched and pinched the pages between pointer and thumb, the soft texture of the paper seeming to cut into his skin.

Glennon's eyes tracked the words on the page. It wasn't right. How was this right? How was he holding his own letter?

Today, we stepped onto Isle Philippeaux, and everything inside me felt sick, he read in his handwriting. Tilting the page a little, he found an arrow pointing to a long note that trailed from the top corner of the page and down the margins of the paper.

Not EVERYTHING inside you can FEEL sick, Glennon. Use precise language when you write. If you're not clear, your audience will NOT understand what you mean. You first must master writing for strict communication purposes before you dip into figurative language, especially considering that figurative language is still out of your reach. You are not a good writer.

This time, when Glennon dropped the paper, he didn't grab it back up again. He could read it just fine, sitting this close to the ground. He could even read it fine *laying* on the ground. He could read it from beneath the table, where he'd scooted his body, trying to get away from the overhead chandelier that shone too-bright light on the pages of his writing. He could read it curled into a ball with his eyes smashed shut, for the page had been copied onto the back of his lids.

His father had marked up the entire letter in red ink, as if Glennon were one of his college students who had failed an assignment.

"I wrote that for myself." Glennon's lips were wet with tears, and when he spoke, his words turned to mush. "I wrote that for myself. I didn't mean to send it to Dad. I got my two piles of writing mixed up. I made a mistake—it was a *mistake*."

At the very bottom of the last page of the writing Glennon had created just for himself, just for his own enjoyment, was a last note from his dad.

Please stick to factual writing, Glen. You are not one of the greats of literature, and you certainly won't be if you continue to write as you have here.

"I never wanted to be great," he said, sighing out the words on a sob, as the parts of himself that had felt whole a moment before cracked in half. "I just wanted to be myself."

Glennon broke then. It took so much work to hold himself in one piece all the time, and now, he lost the ability. A gaping hole opened inside him, and from it flooded sadness and fear—*so much fear*—until it filled Third Keeper's house and lapped beneath him, a pool of his dad's disappointment that froze his skin and drowned his body and made shudders run through his muscles.

From behind, he felt the warmth of his sister's arms. She hugged him, held him against the sadness and anger and *why does the world have to end and then end again and then end all over again?* Because sometimes, that's what it felt like—living with their dad felt like experiencing the end of the world every day in the smallest of ways.

Lee held him...but then suddenly, she left, and he lay on the floor beneath the table on his own. He understood then why she always hid when she panicked. The chairs around him and the tabletop over him were comforting. Something about seeing all the corners of the box he'd tucked himself into made him feel safe. He knew everything that existed beneath the table with him.

Pencil scratched on paper, and after long moments of

Glennon breathing hard, he heard the sound of a sheaf of paper being slid in front of him. He didn't dare open his eyes—nothing in him would survive reading his dad's critique again—but when Lee didn't say anything or push him, he blinked his salty, wet eyelids open.

Today, we stepped onto Isle Philippeaux, and everything inside me felt sick. The isle seems to have wedged something in me, almost as if my heart and lungs have decided to feel homesick and seasick permanently.

No red lines. None of his dad's comments. Just Glennon's words in his sister's swooping handwriting.

Glennon cried now with Lee's papers tucked against his chest, because as horrible as his dad made him feel, his sister made him feel the opposite. He crawled from beneath the table, staying on his hands and knees to follow after Lee. He found her sitting cross-legged before the fire, holding his original papers above the flame.

"May I burn them?" Lee asked.

Glennon nodded, and Lee set the letter inside the blaze.

The papers burned, and he couldn't tell the difference between the fire eating at the letter and the fire eating at his dad's disappointment. Both were consumed just the same.

"For what it's worth, I think what you wrote is beautiful. It reads like a good story," Lee said. "I like good stories."

"You like scary stories."

"I like all stories, especially ones written by my brother. I didn't know you liked to write."

Glennon shrugged. He folded himself onto the comfy couch beside the fire, running his fingers over Lee's handwriting. She settled herself on the ground before him, with her spine pressed to his shins.

"Did you know that I like to pretend to make movies?" Lee said.

"No."

"I do. Sometimes I like to think about the future. I'll live far away from home, and I'll make movies for real. I wish I could make them now with Cassandra and Lawrence, but Dad would never let me borrow the camera recorder."

"Why does he hate us so much?" Glennon whispered.

"I think Dad loves us." Lee's fingers marched up the side of her head and covered her ears in the way she did when she didn't feel good. "Except…when Mom says she loves us, she says it like, *I'll listen to you talk about all the things you love,* but when Dad says he loves us, he says it like, *I'll let you listen to me talk about all the things I love.* I don't know why it's different, but it is."

Glennon didn't know what to say to this. He wondered how much Lee had thought about the question of their parents and how they loved them or how they hated them. He always did his best to *never* think about it. It hurt too much.

Floorboards creaked in the kitchen, then the dining room, and last the living room, and Uncle Job's shadow stretched long over the couch, wavering a bit in the light of the fire. He bent down a little and handed both Glennon and Lee plates piled up with baked beans and mac 'n' cheese. He met Glennon's gaze, not commenting on Glennon's face that was puffy and sore and streaked with tears.

This time when Glennon cried, he did it because he realized that Uncle Job's love said something like, *You can cry, and it's okay.* And in front of him, Lee's love said, *I will listen to you, and I will believe you, and I will stand beside you.*

Both of those loves healed the broken parts of him, just a little.

Uncle Job left for his evening work shift as soon as they finished eating. Glennon and Lee sat facing one another in front of the fire. Seamus curled over Lee's feet, legs stretched before him, head tipped back and eyes closed against the warmth of the fire. While he baked, Glennon and Lee made plans. The major problem was that neither of them really knew what stopped ghosts or even how to tell who was a ghost.

Townsend and Everett were, but what about other people on the island? What were they supposed to do—go around pointing the mirror at everyone and see if they shifted forms?

"These aren't the same sort of ghosts as in *Poltergeist*," Lee said.

"Movies probably aren't good sources of research," said Glennon.

"Probably not." Lee looked up at him, careful not to disturb Seamus when she moved. "Do you know what I like about scary movies?"

"That they're scary?"

"No. Well…yeah, I like that they're scary. But I like more that they always tell me that bad things end and bad guys can be defeated."

"Don't a *lot* of people usually die in scary movies?" Glennon had seen enough of Lee's movies to know that they didn't always end well for people.

Lee shrugged, probably thinking the same thing as Glennon—if they were in a scary movie right now, which of them wouldn't make it out alive?

Glennon's gaze drifted toward the stairs in the direction of their mother. He didn't like that she still slept, still didn't feel well, and also that they didn't really understand why or how to fix it.

"We need to do more research," he said.

"We need a library," Lee said.

Glennon's memory flashed back to the other day when they were in town. "Miss Lacey!"

"Who?"

"There's a library on the island. I met the librarian, Miss Lacey, at the post office. She was picking up a huge order of books. She said to come by if I ever needed a book. Maybe she has something on ghosts!"

Lee paused halfway through the motion of gliding her hand down Seamus's back. "That's a really good idea."

"Thanks." Glennon reached out to pet Seamus too, but the cat jerked back as soon as Glennon touched him. Seamus hissed and slunk away, moving closer to the fire and farther from Glennon.

"Although, I'm not sure we should outright ask Miss Lacey if she knows of any ghosts, personally." Without Seamus there to keep Lee's hands busy, she picked at a seam on her shirt. "What if she's in league with them?"

"With Townsend and Everett?"

"And the thing that tried to drown you."

Glennon glanced at the fire. The flames shifted and grew,

fluttering this way and that, as if in time to the beat of a heart. He recoiled. "Right. And the thing that tried to drown me."

"We'll go to the library in the morning," Lee said. She took a pillow from the couch and curled her body around Seamus, both of them soaking in the warmth of the fire.

Glennon headed to bed. In the quiet of the creaking third bedroom in the Third Keeper's house, his mind stretched out, and he considered the whole of Isle Philippeaux and everyone on it. That night, he didn't write a letter to his dad.

All he wrote in his notebook was:

Who else knows about the ghosts on Isle Philippeaux?

19

In the morning, Glennon hardly wanted to climb out of bed. The bones in his chest still ached and deep exhaustion lingered in his muscles. What got him out of bed were thoughts of Mom and how her exhaustion seemed so much worse than his.

In her room, she had the blinds pulled over the window and the room cloaked in darkness. He moved carefully through the gloomy space until he stood a few feet from her bed.

"She's sleeping a lot," Lee whispered from the doorway. "Do you remember the time she didn't get out of bed for a week, and she wasn't sick? She didn't have a fever or anything. When she finally did get out of bed, all she cooked for dinner was tomato soup? Just tomato soup for like…a month."

The memory of that month sunk inside him, dropping heavy inside his chest. He joined Lee in the doorway and said, "Dad complained."

"Dad complained and Mom still made tomato soup. I don't think she smiled once that whole time."

"I don't like talking about this." He hadn't been able to help Mom at all during that time. Nothing he did made things better. He hadn't been able to keep her safe from the sadness, not at all.

Lee huffed.

Despite the discomfort of talking, Glennon made himself say, "She was really sad, and it was really scary."

"I'm glad she got better."

"But don't you think…I think that sadness is still inside her somewhere. I can see it on her face sometimes."

Lee turned to him, eyes wide. "I didn't know you'd noticed that."

Surprised, Glennon said, "Do you think the same thing is happening now?"

"Do you?"

Glennon said firmly, "No. She's only sad like that when we're at home. She's never sad when we go other places, and she hasn't been as sad since we've been here. I think this is happening because of Everett."

"That means we have to stop him."

"Are we going to town?" Uncle Job asked, interrupting them. He stood in the open front door at the bottom of the stairs. Lee had asked him earlier in the morning to give them a ride. "You'll want to wear a thick coat. It's cold out today."

Glennon pulled his windbreaker out of the front closet and layered it over his jean jacket. Lee stuffed her arms into a puffy coat a shade of orange so bright it made Glennon's eyes hurt. She opened the door, and dry air the temperature of Superior's waters crept through the threshold. Glennon almost doubled back for his own winter jacket, but by then Uncle Job sat in the car with the top of his head touching the ceiling.

Silence stretched through the insides of the Camry as they rode into town. It wasn't the heavy, uncomfortable sort of silence Glennon felt when he drove to baseball games with his dad. It felt more like hiding inside a blanket fort and writing secret stories in his journal on a rainy Saturday. All cozy and easy. His mind didn't scramble for anything to say.

Town was packed as always, people crowding the streets and walking into stores and...*where* did everyone *live*? Maybe there was a whole complex of houses somewhere on the isle that they hadn't driven past before. On the scenic highway, there weren't any roads that shot out toward neighborhoods or apartment complexes.

Uncle Job stopped the car before the library, saying he'd be back in an hour after he finished running errands of his own.

"Do you think he's tired?" Lee asked. "He worked all night."

"I think he would've told us if he were too tired to drive us to town," Glennon said when they stood before the library doors. "Actually, I don't think he would have. He's like Grandma was, remember? Sometimes when Grandma would play board games with us, she would yawn so big. She'd be so tired, but she always refused to take breaks. She'd stay up and play games and get all droopy."

"I miss Grandma." Lee wrenched open the big door to the library and ducked into the warmth of the building.

"She was a good grandma," Glennon said, following her inside.

The library itself was made of a silence similar to what had filled the car with Uncle Job. Glennon felt so comfortable inside it, a smile warmed his face.

Miss Lacey stood behind a desk at the front of the library, easy to spot in a bright blue dress with a white collar sewn along the neckline and at her wrists. The red scar, the one that looked like the branches of an oak tree, peeked from beneath her sleeve and crossed over her right hand. She smiled when she saw him and said, "I was hoping you would come by! Can I help you find a book?"

Glennon cleared his throat, blushing a little at the attention she showered on him. "We're not really here for a book. We don't—we really only read for schoolwork."

"You...what?" Miss Lacey asked, voice tilting upward nearly a whole octave.

"My dad says we're only supposed to read things that make us smarter," Glennon said.

Miss Lacey's smile dropped straight off her face. "What on earth does the word *smarter* mean?"

Glennon felt his own face pinch together, and he had the feeling that both he and Miss Lacey wore the same exact confused expression. "Smarter means…your brain holds more information. More facts."

"So, you're saying your dad only wants you reading books like the encyclopedia? Are you supposed to memorize the dictionary?"

Glennon had the feeling Miss Lacey was mocking his dad somehow, but he couldn't figure out why.

"The encyclopedia is a very worthy sort of book to look through, if you need it for a specific purpose," Miss Lacey said. "But there are many other sorts of books that are just as worthy of being read."

Racking his brain, Glennon tried to come up with the authors his dad taught about in his teaching job. He came up short, not able to think of any, even though he knew his dad had lectured him about them many times before. "He just… he wants us to read books that teachers assign for schoolwork."

"That's ridiculous. You should read whatever makes you happy. If what makes you happy are the books your teachers assign, then read those books, but otherwise, find new worlds to dive into! Stories to swim inside of! Read and experience other people's lives, even if those people are different from you. Sometimes, those are the best stories to read." Miss Lacey gently set down the book she held, but then she pressed both her hands flat onto the counter, hard enough to change the color of her knuckles. "One of my favorite recent books is the delightfully titled *Howl's Moving Castle* by Diana Wynne Jones, and I know for a fact that none of your teachers will assign it. It might very well be a book you would devour. Stories exist for you to escape inside of, for whatever reason you may need. Truly, there are many ways we can become smarter while reading. It's for you to decide what sort of smarter you'd like to be."

Glennon blushed even more furiously than he had before. Why did people have to keep telling him about the word *smart*?

"I like scary stories," Lee said.

"*Ohh*, so do I!" Miss Lacey leaned a bit over the counter in her excitement. "Have you read Mary Downing Hahn's books? She writes ghost stories. They're quite spooky."

Lee shook her head. "I really only watch scary movies. I didn't know there were scary books too."

"I'm so glad you came to me." Miss Lacey turned, bustling out from behind the counter.

"Me too," Glennon said back, happier than he'd been in… maybe ever.

Lee held out one hand to Glennon and gave him a sharp look that said, *Stay focused; remember why we came here.* She said, "Would you mind pointing us in the direction of the encyclopedias? We actually do have research to do, and I think the encyclopedia would be the right book for it."

Miss Lacey drooped a bit, as if she were sad not to show them to the spooky book aisle. She gestured for them to follow her. When they stood before the row of Encyclopedia Britannica books, she asked, "What are you interested in reading about?"

Glennon said, "Gho—"

Lee elbowed his side, making him grunt, and she said, "Government. We're doing a project for school on types of government."

One of Miss Lacey's soft smiles took over her mouth. Glennon was starting to get used to the pleasantness of that smile. "Government is a wonderful topic of research. One should always understand what sort of governance they're under." She pulled out one of the encyclopedias and handed it to Lee.

Thumping down to sit right in the middle of the aisle, Lee flipped to the section on *Ghosts* while Miss Lacey walked to the end of the aisle where a stack of books sat on a cart. She started placing them back on the shelves where they belonged.

Glennon sat beside his sister, close enough that she could whisper without allowing anyone else to overhear them.

"Listen," Lee said, one finger following along the words as she read. "*Ghosts often appear how they looked while living, though they may also take other forms. The form itself is believed to be the human spirit that separated from the body after death. Ghosts may haunt one of several things: a person they have a connection to, a place they have a connection to, or an object they have a connection to. This exists because of a strong emotional connection. Ghosts may have abilities that include moving objects, taking on different forms, creating disembodied sounds, affecting weather patterns, among others.*"

When she stopped reading, Glennon scanned over the entry again, then asked, "If Everett is haunting Mom...why? He doesn't have a strong emotional connection to her. He just met her!"

"It doesn't make sense." Lee closed the heavy book, the cover thumping shut. "None of this makes sense. I hate when things don't make sense!"

Glennon snatched the unhelpful encyclopedia from Lee and shoved it back onto the shelf. He sat down again and waited for one of them to come up with the next course of action or the next place to look in the library for more information on ghosts. Giving his hands something to do, he dug in the pocket of his windbreaker and pulled out the compact mirror Keeper Sanz had given him.

"This showed Townsend's true form." The little gold latch on the front was nothing more than a tiny button, a sliver of metal that easily popped open when he pressed it with his thumb. "But Keeper Sanz said it would show the true form of Isle Philippeaux."

"What are we supposed to do? Point the mirror at the isle? See if the dirt will change into something else?" Lee asked.

"What's an isle supposed to change into?"

"A cat," Lee joked.

"Seamus." Glennon snorted. "Maybe Isle Philippeaux's been Seamus all along."

Lee scooted next to him, and he held up the mirror. Both their faces squashed together in the reflection, their dark blue eyes matching one another's exactly.

"At least we know we're not ghosts," Lee said.

"Maybe we can find the right book with it." Glennon angled the mirror around, the titles of the books behind him flipping around in the reflection. They didn't change or take on another form, though, and they certainly didn't tell Glennon if they were the "right" book to read.

His hand wavered a bit, and Miss Lacey walked into view behind them. She held a pile of books in one arm, and with the other, she pushed a metal cart.

Glennon choked on the air he breathed. His hand trembled,

but he locked his wrist and held the mirror steady. Miss Lacey's blue dress with white collar now appeared tattered in the mirror. It fluttered over the creature that now stood inside it.

Harsh light sparked at the edges of what had once been Miss Lacey's human form.

"*Ohh,*" Lee said on a long sigh. "She's *beautiful.*"

Miss Lacey stopped moving. The air inside the library turned from summertime warmth to the-bottom-of-Superior cold, dropping at once and frosting the tip of Glennon's nose. He snapped the mirror shut and spun, assuming Miss Lacey would transform back human when he put away the compact, just like Townsend had.

But no, Miss Lacey the ghost creature stood behind them with wind whipping in a tight funnel around her. Air wrapped the cloth of her blue dress tightly against her body, except her body was made from harsh droplets of rain and splinters of shredded steel. It snatched up her hair that was now made from thin metal shavings. The shards flew out, reminding Glennon of the snakes on Medusa's head, all writhing and hissing at Glennon and Lee.

"WHO ARE YOU TO DEMAND I TAKE THIS FORM?" Miss Lacey cried, her voice made from the grind of metal skidding against metal.

Lee flinched and covered her ears.

Glennon grasped the back of his sister's coat and dragged her backward. This wasn't at all what had happened with Townsend—Townsend might have looked like a monster, but she hadn't *turned into* one.

"I DO NOT CHOOSE TO TAKE THIS FORM. THIS FORM IS NOT MINE." She stole toward them, slow, one step at a time, and as she did, she expanded. "WHO ARE YOU TO BRING A MIRROR TO THIS PLACE AND FORCE ME TO TAKE A FORM I DID NOT CHOOSE FOR MYSELF?"

Wind whipped around them and grabbed at the edges of their clothes. Lee's wind sprites, but a thousand times more hostile.

"I DO NOT CHOOSE THIS FORM. *I DO NOT CHOOSE IT!*" Miss Lacey screamed, her words the same as a crack of thunder. The sound popped the air around them, vacuuming all other noise in Miss Lacey's direction.

Air zipped toward Miss Lacey, dragging Glennon and Lee with it. They dug their heels into the thin carpet of the library. Glennon screamed and the iron taste of blood covered the back of his tongue.

He snatched a book off the shelf and hurled it at Miss Lacey. It shot toward her, and then *through* her—a hole gaping open in her center. She took a book from a shelf, as well, and held it in one hand. The cover fell open. One by one, the pages tore free from the book and flung back in Glennon and Lee's direction.

"We need to run," he shouted. He had no idea if Lee heard his words. *He* couldn't hear his own words over the storm that filled the library. He fastened his hand around Lee's and pulled.

They ran. The library door stood open—they'd never closed it—and they burst into the winter-cold day. They pelted toward a corner in the road. Before they skidded around the turn, Glennon glanced back at the library. Miss Lacey stood in the doorway, arms stretched out and fingers clawing over the threshold. The scar on her hand stood out, fizzing with brightness, until all at once, the light shot out and seared straight into the sky. A lightning bolt poured out of Miss Lacey's body. It crashed through the clouds, spiderwebbing in every direction.

Glennon and Lee turned and ran again, even faster than before.

"YOU CANNOT MAKE US TAKE THESE FORMS, NOT WITHOUT COST." Miss Lacey's voice and their own terror chased them down the street. "*NOT WITHOUT COST.*"

20

Glennon didn't last long running. He'd never liked running.
I'll run when a bear chases me, he'd always joked to his friends.
Turned out, he could run real fast when a ghost chased him,
and now that the ghost wasn't chasing him, he had to quit. He
came to a stop and folded in half, hands coming to his knees
while he heaved.

"That was…I don't—*what just happened*?" He gasped, his
mind faltering just like his speech.

Beside him, Lee's body heaved in the shivering, scared way
it often did, sounding as if it'd forgotten how to properly suck
air into her lungs.

He sat on the ground and held out one arm. She curled up
against him. He said, "It was loud. So, so loud. It was a jump
scare. I don't like jump scares in real life." Lee covered her ears
with her hands. "I don't know why I get so scared."

It was scary. I think when things are scary, you're supposed
to be scared. We didn't know Miss Lacey would be a ghost.

Looking up to take stock of their surroundings, Glennon immediately wished he were anywhere else but in the middle of town.

They were surrounded by people.

He leaned close to Lee's ear and whispered, "It can't be coincidence that Townsend and Everett and the ghost in the water that tried to drown me *and* Miss Lacey are all ghosts." He pulled out the compact mirror from his pocket and clasped it in one hand, as if it could protect him, although all it'd done so far was get him into trouble.

Lee closed her hand over Glennon's. "If you open the mirror, we don't know who else will transform. *Anyone* could be a ghost. We have no idea who's alive and who's not!"

Would all these people transform if he opened the mirror? Would only some of them? If so, would they be kind, like Townsend, or would they attack them, like Miss Lacey?

They sat on a curb alongside the road that wound by the shipyard. Around them teemed sailors and dock workers and men who wore outfits Glennon knew didn't belong in the 1980s. They didn't even belong in the 1950s. He peered closer, spotting the backward way some of them moved, the shadowy scars that marred their faces and hands, the otherworldly wind that tousled hair and tugged at coats. He noticed too how some wore no coats at all and didn't seem bothered by the freezing temperatures.

Why had he not noticed any of this before?

"Taking a sit-down?" asked a man with a gruff voice. His face was shielded with a flat-brimmed hat that encircled his whole head and shaded his eyes. "I'd like to take a sit-down too."

Glennon tightened his arm over Lee's shoulders.

"But, you see, I can't remember the last time I was allowed a break from my work." He rubbed one palm across his chin. "Forty years? Fifty? One hundred eighty-two? Time is confusing."

"*Shh*, you'll upset them," said a woman behind him. She swatted at his shoulders. "And they're already so upset. Look at them. They look like they've seen a ghost."

The man chortled, and the woman laughed. Laughed and *laughed* as if she'd told a joke so funny, she'd laugh about it for days.

"I know I shouldn't scare you." The man bent low. He raised his hand to the brim of his hat. "At least not before The Waning. I shouldn't scare you, but…" He pushed up his hat, but beneath it lay an expanse of shadows. Where his eyes should have been was nothing but gaping, red-tinged holes.

Glennon nearly swallowed his tongue to keep from whimpering aloud. In the background, the woman still laughed. The man reached toward Glennon. Something dark and sticky dripped down his cheeks. *A ghost.*

But then, another body pushed in front of the ghost with no eyes. "Begone!" the man yelled in a commanding voice. He shook something silver and glinting in one fist.

Startled, the ghost-man and ghost-woman cringed away. Their forms flickered. The human bodies they wore dropped away, revealing creatures Glennon couldn't quite comprehend—creatures like Townsend and Miss Lacey that were made of wind and storms and rain. They turned and ran down the street, their human forms popping back as they escaped from the tinfoil the man held.

He turned.

"Gibraltar!" Glennon stood, wanting to reach out and hug the sailor.

He grabbed Glennon's shoulders. "Have you figured out a way off the island?"

"No! No. The ferry isn't runny anymore." Glennon scrambled to think; there wasn't a way off Isle Philippeaux, except... "Townsend has a boat. It's little. Just a small fishing boat."

"Townsend," Gibraltar muttered.

"At Ingram Lighthouse. You were there the other day. I saw you."

Gibraltar gave one firm nod. He released Glennon's arms. "Whatever you do, don't let them steal your soul."

Glennon stumbled at the sudden release of Gibraltar's strong grip.

"Keep your soul protected. If they rip it out of you, they'll bury it where you won't be able to find it again." Gibraltar reached into one pocket and pulled out a square of tinfoil. He pressed it against Glennon's chest—right where the bruise bloomed—and then, he disappeared into the crowd.

"We need to find Uncle Job," Glennon said, voice shaking.

Beside him, Lee didn't speak. He pulled her up so she stood, and together, they went to find their uncle.

21

Lee's voice broke. "I w-want Seamus. He helps. Seamus always makes me feel better."

Glennon wound them around the outer edge of the shipyard, all the while keeping his eye on the strange sailors around them. Beyond, ships clogged the bay. One in particular snagged his view. The bright red paint of its hull was unmistakable, as well as the blocky white letters of her name: the *Anabeth*.

Words came to him then, sudden and quick, a memory of his mother singing: "'*Superior, they said, 'never gives up her dead when the gales of November come early.*'"

"What?" Lee said.

He lifted one quivering finger and pointed at the ship. It floated on the water, whole and unmarred. Lee took the mirror he still clutched in his hand. She snapped it open and held it up so it captured the ship in its reflection. Its image warped, a jagged crack splitting up its side, water billowing and filling its interior, the steel groaning as it bent and twisted.

Lee closed the mirror and the moment ended. The *Anabeth* became whole once again.

"Is everything a ghost?" Glennon asked.

They scurried away from the shipyard. Panic made them move fast. As they headed away from the bay, the road became less and less crowded until they were the only ones left.

"Why did we never see any of this before?" Lee asked. "Why did we never see ghost people or ghost ships or ghost anything? All I knew is that something weird was happening; I didn't know it'd be *ghosts*."

Glennon kept glancing over his shoulder. The aching sense that they were being followed filled him. They took a turn in the road, and there stood Kit. His shoulders stooped, a deep sadness seeming to sit heavy on his back. He was still stuck here, without his family. Did he know about the ghosts? Should Glennon tell him? If he did, would Kit tell him he was making things up?

Glennon was suddenly very grateful that he'd never seen Kit with Everett. He didn't know what Kit had been doing during the days, but he was glad it didn't include spending time with the ghost and getting his soul ripped out.

"It's busy down by the shipyard, what with everyone working and getting ready for The Waning," Kit said when they approached. "Probably isn't safe for anyone to be down there."

"*That's* why it's so busy!" Glennon said. "Everyone's getting ready for The Waning tomorrow." They were supposed to be gone by then, and besides, he still didn't know what The Waning actually was.

Lee glanced behind her, back where people milled about. "What sort of celebration is it though? Why has Uncle Job never told us about it?"

"Maybe he doesn't really know," Glennon said. "He's never been here for it. Maybe he doesn't care much about the celebration."

"We can ask him when we find wherever he disappeared to," Lee said.

Kit rubbed his forehead hard, leaving red marks on his skin. "Have you tried the cemetery? It's big. Right in the middle of town. I think I saw him there earlier." Shifting directions, he led them down a road and onto a quieter side street.

A low stone wall appeared out of nowhere, and inside it was the cemetery. Lush green grass swooped over a long field that was interrupted by tombstones and carved angels and a mausoleum in the center. In the distance, Glennon found Uncle Job's unmistakable figure standing hunched over a grave.

Who had died here that Uncle Job wanted to visit?

Glennon turned say thank you to Kit, but he'd already walked away, and Glennon found himself waving at Kit's back.

The next time Glennon found him, he'd need to tell him about the ghosts and try to get Kit to stay with them. He wanted Kit to escape Isle Philippeaux at the same time they did.

"What are you doing?" Lee asked.

"I wanted…" Glennon could no longer find where Kit had gone. "Never mind."

"Why are there so many graves?" Lee asked, pointing at the multitude of headstones. "If most of the people we've seen on the island have been ghosts, why would they have graves? They can't have all died and been buried here, right? Lots of them would have died out on the lake while sailing. If that's the case, then are these graves empty?"

Glennon had no response for that, except to continue walking toward their uncle.

When they approached, Uncle Job was hunched over, elbows tucked close to his body and chin tucked close to his chest. He peered down at a grave with a small stone propped at the top. He looked sad and quiet and not at all like the Uncle Job they'd come to know over the past months of living with him.

The graveyard *felt* like death. It wasn't death that felt like an ending, though, or even a continuation of something. This was death that was…Glennon didn't have a word for it. It felt like finding a still pond in the center of a forest in the heat of summer, algae growing on top, the scent of rot and mildew steaming from its center. The thick feel of it hung in the air and seemed to waft around Uncle Job in a halo. His dark hair fluttered even though the wind hadn't blown since Glennon and Lee had left Miss Lacey.

Lee's legs gave out beneath her. She sat down on the ground, hard, and when Glennon looked at her, he saw fat tears rolling down her cheeks.

"Lee?" he asked.

She pointed at Uncle Job, then whispered, "Why would a ghost need a grave?"

"What do you mean—" Glennon stopped himself talking. This time when words left him, it wasn't because he was scared or felt stupid, it was because despair washed through his body.

All this time, they'd been trying to find out what sort of monster Everett was, but what if Uncle Job was one of those monsters too? What if Uncle Job was a ghost?

It didn't make any sense.

Glennon steeled his spine and continued on until he stood at the grave beside his uncle. He said, "We met a lot of ghosts today."

Tears rolled down Uncle Job's cheeks, just like Lee's. They wet the thick beard that grew over his chin.

"You're a ghost too." Glennon's throat tightened around

the words. Anger and confusion and sadness washed through him. He'd been searching for answers, when all this time, an answer had lived inside the same house as him. How had Uncle Job died without Glennon knowing? Did Mom know?

Uncle Job's glossy gaze met his. He wiped at his tears and nodded once, slow. "I wanted to tell you."

The stone before them read Uncle Job's name, though there was no inscription below it.

"Can you write something on it?" Glennon asked, quiet, thinking of Christopher Picard's tombstone and the sad message that had been scrawled on it.

Uncle Job stooped, his spine folding beneath Glennon's question. "I haven't decided yet."

"Kit told me that the graves here aren't known for their ability to give the dead rest."

"No, they aren't."

"He said there's lots of gallows humor on the tombstones."

"There is," Uncle Job agreed.

"You're nice though." A flood of emotions washed through Glennon. His mouth trembled, muscles pulling hard at his lips. "I think you should write something nice on your grave. *Kept safe those who needed safekeeping.* Something like that."

With tears still leaking from his eyes, Uncle Job rested one massive arm over Glennon's shoulders, said, "Thank you," and into the blank stone appeared words in a slow scrawl, as if carved by a ghostly hand:

JOB JOHNSON

1955–1989

KEPT SAFE THOSE WHO NEEDED
SAFEKEEPING

22

A pit had unfurled inside of Glennon when he realized Uncle Job was a ghost, and it refused to close. It gaped open, sucking down the last bits of happiness he had. He'd begun the day by believing Everett was the monster, but then they'd met Miss Lacey. They'd seen the ghosts in the shipyard. They'd learned their uncle was, apparently, dead.

Everyone on Isle Philippeaux was a ghost. Everyone except for the McCues, Kit, and Gibraltar.

Lee sat in the front passenger seat while Uncle Job drove them back to Graving. Glennon sat in the middle of the back seat so he could lean forward over the console and pretend he was in the front. Usually when he sat in the back, he'd spend time thinking, but today, he didn't want to think. He didn't want to be left alone inside his mind.

"Everyone is a ghost," Glennon said.

Uncle Job gave a small nod, and the pit inside Glennon grew even more cavernous.

Glennon dug in his pocket and pulled out the compact mirror that had made Miss Lacey turn into a screaming tunnel of wind and lightning, and asked, "May I look at you in the mirror?"

Uncle Job took his eyes off the road long enough to make Glennon uncomfortable. He said, "I'd prefer if you wouldn't."

"You don't like the ghost form?" Lee asked.

"It's not a matter of liking, it's…" Uncle Job took in a deep breath. "I don't know how to explain it."

Glennon understood not knowing how to explain something. "Does the ghost form hurt?"

"No. I'm dead. I don't feel pain, at least not in the same way I did when I was alive. It's more like a deep hunger."

"You eat food though," Lee said.

Uncle Job smiled, though his eyes stayed sad. "I do. People who have been dead longer typically don't, like First Keeper. They stop remembering they needed food when they were alive. I haven't forgotten yet."

"What are you hungry for, then, if it isn't food?" Glennon asked.

Uncle Job's smile drifted away. His mouth stayed closed, no ready answer for Glennon's question.

"It doesn't make any sense!" Lee shouted, startling both Glennon and Uncle Job. She punched one fist against her thigh.

"It doesn't make any sense. We got a letter from you. You said there'd been an accident at the lighthouse, but that you were okay. You said you were being transferred to Isle Philippeaux, and you invited us to visit! You'd gotten hurt, but you were okay!" She waved her hands at Uncle Job, then at the whole isle around them. "Being a ghost isn't *being okay!*"

"I didn't write that letter," Uncle Job said.

Glennon stared at Uncle Job, at the lines in his face that were carved by days spent in the sun and evenings spent in Lake Superior's storms. He had no idea how to respond to what his uncle had just said.

"You...what?" Lee said.

"I didn't write that letter," he said.

"Then who did?"

Uncle Job tightened his hands around the steering wheel. "I'm not sure I'm able to tell you."

"Was it Everett? Did Everett write the letter?" Glennon asked.

"Uncle Job!" Lee said. "Please. We need to know."

"No."

"*Uncle Job!*"

"*NO!*" An unearthly, inhuman sound came through Uncle Job's voice, the crackling smoke of a fire and the pain that came when drinking a too hot cup of cocoa and getting burnt.

Unease prickled through Glennon. Tension pulled his body taut. Beside him, Lee sucked in her breath. They both held themselves still, watching Uncle Job...waiting for him to unleash his anger. Anxiety zipped tight the muscles in Glennon's body, his lungs refused to fully inflate.

"This isle is not an easy thing to talk about." Otherworldly pops and snaps hid inside Uncle Job's voice, reminding Glennon of Miss Lacey right before her anger ripped through the library... and of his dad's voice right before he threw words sharpened to the point of daggers at his family...right before he called Glennon stupid and incompetent and worthless.

Uncle Job shook his head, his gaze trained on the road. "None of this is easy to talk about. *Death* isn't easy to talk about, especially when it's your own. I'm sorry."

Glennon hadn't known they were asking about Uncle Job's death. He'd thought they were talking about the monsters on the island. All of his questions piled inside him: *What was death like? What was the afterlife? Why was he on Isle Philippeaux? Why were all the ghosts on Isle Philippeaux? If Uncle Job hadn't written the letter to Glennon's mom, then who had? If they hadn't received that letter, would the McCues have traveled to Isle Philippeaux at all?*

Two questions loomed bigger than all the rest: Did Mom know Uncle Job was dead? And...was Mom a ghost too? What if that's why she'd been acting so strange?

Glennon curled in the back seat, his thoughts racing through each of his questions, and all the while, he waited for Uncle Job's anger to explode. He realized that not once in all the time he'd known his uncle had he ever let loose his anger. And yet, Glennon always found himself waiting for it.

That was the thing with anger. Sometimes, there was no indication it was about to erupt. That's why Glennon always had to be prepared for it.

Except he was *never* ready. Never.

He waited and waited, spending the rest of the car ride watching the posture of Uncle Job's body, the way he breathed, the tone of voice with which he talked.

Uncle Job had been angry…he *was* angry, but that anger never reached out to hurt Glennon. The pain of it never came, and it made Glennon wonder—what was anger when it didn't come with glass explosions and furious fists and words designed to break?

What was anger when it didn't exist to hurt?

⌒

When they drove up to Graving, the lighthouse's beam shone into the day. *On-off, on-off, on-on-off* went its steady, predictable, comforting rhythm. Why was the light on before it got dark?

"They must be anticipating bad weather," Uncle Job said,

murmuring to himself more than talking out loud, as he parked and climbed from the car. He seemed to flicker, fading out of view, then popping back clearer than before, almost like a highlighter had been traced around his edges. He walked around the Third Keeper's house and headed straight to Graving.

Why hadn't Uncle Job been flickering before today? Had there always been clues that he was a ghost, and Glennon had ignored them?

"We have to tell Mom he's a ghost," Glennon said from the back seat.

"There's no way Mom will believe us." Lee tucked her chin into her jacket. "Doubt and denial is always part of scary stories. People don't want to believe when bad things happen to them. Besides, sometimes the scary thing in the story works *really* hard to make people believe everything's okay or that the bad things are only in their heads. The monster tries to make people believe it's not a monster."

"Everett never tried very hard to make us believe he wasn't a monster," Glennon said. "Mom would believe if Uncle Job showed her his ghost form."

"What makes you think he'd show anyone his ghost form? He could hardly talk about being a ghost, and he wanted nothing to do with your mirror."

Frustrated, Glennon asked, "Why are we here, Lee? Why

did we get a letter about Isle Philippeaux if Uncle Job never sent it to us?"

Lee tapped her fingers against her knees. "Uncle Job's always seemed so confused over us ending up here. If he didn't send us the letter, he probably didn't know we were coming. We probably showed up on his doorstep out of the blue."

Glennon scrambled to think back. Mom's decision to move them north had been last minute. She'd said she was going to try and stay home for once while their dad was away, but then she'd received the letter from Uncle Job. He'd made Isle Philippeaux seem like a nice, quiet island, so she'd packed them up and they'd gone to live at the Third Keeper's doorstep. Glennon couldn't remember if she'd actually talked with him on the phone before they'd arrived. Uncle Job had never seemed particularly happy about their presence at Graving. Glennon had assumed it was because he was used to living alone and not having two kids running around his house.

"We shouldn't be here." Lee climbed from the car and slammed shut the door. "If Mom had taken two seconds to contact Uncle Job directly, he probably would've told us not to come. We'd be at home, safe."

She stalked toward the Third Keeper's house, but Glennon stayed in the car, hearing her words inside his head. *Home, safe*, she'd said.

When had either of them ever said those two words together?

He left the quiet of the car in favor of checking on Mom. He found Lee standing in front of Mom's door, peering through the open crack. This is what they did during the month when she'd been *sad*. They'd checked on her, even though their dad had yelled, *It's your mother's job to fix herself*, and had slammed the door hard enough to crack it down the side.

Now, though, there was no one around who would yell at them.

The door creaked open, metal hinges complaining over being used, as if they hadn't been opened in decades instead of hours. Inside, one lamp shone beside the bed. The pattern on the shade, a gray and white mosaic, threw shadows across Mom that turned her pallor even more sickly and dewy than it had been before. Tiptoeing inside, they stood over her. The quilt over her chest moved only the very slightest when she breathed.

Fear threaded through Glennon. It was a very different sort of fear than the one that came when his dad was mad. This fear made a small home inside his lungs and pushed against his heart. This fear *hurt*.

He said to Lee, "You don't think she's a ghost, do you? If she died, we'd know it. Right?"

Lee didn't respond.

He sat on the edge of Mom's bed and took out the compact

mirror, his breaths coming in the smallest of wheezes. Dread made his body forget how to work right. The latch popped open, and he looked at his reflection. The thin skin beneath his eyes was a dark shade of blue that reminded him of Lake Superior.

"I can't do it," he said to Lee. He couldn't turn the mirror toward Mom. He was too scared.

Lee reached out and placed her hand over his. Together, they turned the mirror. In its reflection, Mom lay still. Dark smudges rimmed her eyes, just like Glennon's. Limp hair fell across her pillow and the purple and yellow quilt that was pulled up to her chin.

She was whole and human and *not* a ghost.

Relief pushed the fear from Glennon's body and he sagged, but as he did, he caught sight of a faded rope that pooled atop Mom's chest. The fibers of it looked nearly see-through. He leaned closer to the mirror, then turned toward Mom. He was *sure* he hadn't noticed any ropes on top of the quilt.

Sure enough, nothing. No rope, no scratchy fibers piled on her body. He looked in the mirror again. The cable, pale brown and nearly unseeable, stretched toward her chest. At its end was a fishhook that glinted in the dim light of the room. It pierced through her skin and sunk into her ribcage, right over her heart.

"Lee?" he whispered.

He held the mirror at a better angle, wishing it were larger and could show the whole of Mom and the rope. He turned the compact this way and that, revealing the way the rope seemed to disappear into the very center of her body.

Lee grabbed the mirror and did exactly as he'd done, looking at the rope that could only be seen in the mirror's reflection.

"Glennon," Lee's voice, pitched too high, sent creeping shivers straight through to Glennon's bones.

She pressed one finger against the mirror, smudging the surface, and Glennon noticed she pointed the mirror at *him* and not at Mom. He'd seen his own reflection in the mirror before though—he knew he wasn't a ghost! He'd definitely know if he'd ever died!

She angled the compact toward his chest, and inside the silver surface, the room with its feeble lighting barely revealed Glennon's reflection and his own chest...into which dipped a silver fishing hook with a rope tied tightly to its end.

23

Pain exploded in Glennon's chest. He pushed at his skin, breathing shallow so as not to stretch out his ribs and wiggle the fishhook buried inside them.

He snatched the mirror from Lee. The rope appeared only in its glossy surface, a thick, silvery web of tangled thread. It reminded him of something...almost like he'd walked straight into a foggy memory he couldn't quite place. He'd worked so hard to convince himself it was nothing but a bruise, but now that he knew what was hurting him, he couldn't ignore it.

"What is it?" he demanded. "What is it and why don't you have one?"

"It's a rope." Lee fumbled with the quilt over Mom. She searched for the rope there, though of course, she didn't find anything. "I have no idea why I don't have one."

Glennon slammed the mirror shut and gripped it inside his sweaty palm. "My chest has been hurting for days, ever since..."

Lee stopped grappling with the quilt. "Ever since what?"

"I fell off my bike." He touched the tender part of his sternum. "I fell off my bike when it was windy out. I thought I saw someone in the road, and I tried to stop. I ended up crashing. When I got up, I saw Seamus, and I thought he was the one who made me fall. I thought his shadow got tossed up, and it *looked* like a person. What if it wasn't Seamus though? What if I did see a person—what if it was a ghost? What if I biked straight through a ghost?"

"And what? It stuck a rope into you?"

"I guess so, just like the ghost in the waves who tried to throw a rope over me when Townsend took me to Spectre Lighthouse."

"What's the point of it though?" Lee snatched the compact from Glennon and opened it again. She pointed the mirror at Mom's rope, then followed where it led. It pooled off the edge of the bed, lengths of it winding together, and then it trailed along the floor and out the door.

Seamus stood there, right in the middle of the doorway. He raked his claws over the floor and over the rope. When Glennon approached, he hissed, except his large eyes inside his large floofy face locked on Glennon's chest...at the invisible fishhook and rope.

"You knew!" Glennon accused. "You knew about the ghost rope, didn't you? All along, that's why you've hated me this week!"

"Seamus, you good cat!" Lee picked up Seamus, who *meowed*, his cat voice rising and falling as if he were as if he were saying, *of course I knew!* "Have you known about the ghosts this whole time?"

Glennon tried to get near the cat to give him a scratch and say thank you, but of course, Seamus turned away from him.

"We have to follow where the ropes lead," he said.

Lee held Seamus out in front of her. His shoulders hunched toward his chin, his whiskers sticking straight out. "Seamus, we have to go, but *you* have to stay here and protect Mom. Don't let any ghosts put more fishhooks into her."

Seamus kicked his paws and squirmed in Lee's grip. She set him down on top of the rope on Mom. His tail whisked behind him, dusting the quilt, and he picked up one paw, all his sharp claws elongated. It was exactly the same stance he'd taken when he'd stood on Superior's beach; he'd swiped at the water, spearing it straight through.

With the approaching evening and the growing chill, Glennon and Lee dressed in their winter jackets and boots and mittens and grabbed flashlights before leaving. Freezing air blasted them in the face when they opened the front door. The thermometer read thirty degrees.

Glennon opened the mirror and held it out, trying to find the trail of the rope. They headed into the woods, following the path the two ropes made. Above them, the long-limbed, skeletal trees pinned back the bruised sky, the greens and blues mixing together as the sun sank into Superior. Shadows fell deep in the woods, making it difficult to track the ropes with the mirror.

With every step Glennon took, the motion jarred the ache inside his chest. Now that he knew where it came from, it hurt even worse. The pain of it made him scared to breathe; what if he took in too deep of a breath and the fishing hook sank deeper into his bones? All at once, the forest ended. Before them spread an open field with small divots scarring the grass.

The graveyard.

Lee shone her flashlight around the field. The beam highlighted the depressed graves and sunken headstones of the cemetery...and lighted on a rat that sat on top of a carving of an angel. It stared at Lee, then at Glennon.

He took an involuntary step back. The intense feeling of being watched pressed against him from every direction. He shone his own light around, its beam flickering into the wide, green eyes of another rat...and another. They littered the graveyard, and they didn't move a single muscle when they were blinded with the lights.

"I've seen the rats with Everett before." Glennon moved the mirror this way and that, but the rats didn't become tiny whirls of wind and water in its reflection. They weren't ghosts. They were something else entirely.

He held out his flashlight, pointing it right at one. Skin barely covered its bony body. Its skeleton pushed against small tufts of hair that covered its neck and sides. Rot and mildew and something that looked like mold grew over its nose and into its jaw. It didn't twitch or shift at all as Glennon and Lee stared at it.

"Zombie rats," Lee whispered.

"We should go back," Glennon said, but even as he said it, he took a step forward. Retreating wasn't an option, even if they were surrounded by dead rats. They had to find where the ropes led and find a way to save both Mom and him.

The rats tracked Glennon's movement, all shifting their heads at the same time.

"Lee...what do you call it when a bunch of creatures all have the same brain?" He took another step. The rats watched him, the feel of dead eyes sending shivers through to his core.

"Like ant colonies?" Lee placed her feet after his. "Hive mind."

"Yeah, that. *Hive mind.* It's like they're all controlled by one brain. They're controlled by Everett."

"If Everett's controlling them, then that's what we need to worry about, not the rats themselves." Lee walked close enough behind him that he felt her words on the back of his neck. "What is this place?"

"A graveyard," Glennon said. "This is where I ended up after Townsend's ghost story."

"You said Kit was here."

"Yeah, he followed me after I ran. He didn't really seem to like Townsend's story either."

"But he wasn't there."

Glennon crept into the outer edges of the graveyard. "What?"

"He wasn't with us. He wasn't there."

"Yes, he was. He sat right beside me."

Lee shivered, her puffy jacket rustling behind him. "No, he wasn't. Only you, me, and Townsend were sitting by the fire."

"But—"

"I've only ever seen Kit once, on the night of the shipwreck."

Glennon came to a halt. His flashlight brightened over a rat with no eyes in its face, just like the ghost man they'd met that morning. "That doesn't make sense. I've seen him lots of times! On the beach. On the pier. Kit was the one who led us to Uncle Job today. You talked with him!"

"No, I didn't," Lee said with force.

"But, I—"

"I've only seen Kit *once*."

Confusion swept through Glennon. Had no one else besides him seen Kit? Why—how did that make any sense? How was that possible, unless... "Kit's a ghost too, isn't he?"

Suddenly, the ground beneath Glennon dipped and swayed. His knees buckled against the force and he tripped sideways, landing hard on his hip. The rats all squeaked in unison, almost as if they shouted a chaotic word into the night. Wind whipped around the clearing, ripping bits of grass from the earth and shredding the decomposing leaves that still stuck to the ground. The thick scent of dead, mossy things rose into the air. His eyes watered, even though he kept them narrowed against the wind.

Long fingers speared up and broke the surface of a grave. Black light spilled up and through the grass, distorting Glennon's view. The darkness burned his eyes and pulled at something deep inside him, almost as if it were dragging all of the sadness he'd ever felt up and out of his body.

The hand flattened on the hard earth and pulled a body through the surface, dragging bits of dirt up along with it. A fuzzy, brilliant blur ran along the body's edge, making the backs of Glennon's eyeballs ache. It climbed the rest of the way from the grave, tugging its feet free from the earth to stand upright.

This was the ghost that had tried to drown Glennon.

"I hoped you wouldn't figure out that part, at least not until The Waning," said Kit Pike's voice from dead center of the ghostly blur. "Don't you realize, Glennon? We're going to be best friends forever."

24

"Get this rope off me." Glennon was furious for two reasons. First, because Kit held a section of his rope, and second, because Glennon had *liked* Kit.

He'd liked that Kit hadn't seemed to like his dad, just like Glennon. He'd liked that Kit had helped him and been friendly. He'd liked that Kit wanted to be friends. He *didn't* like that Kit was a ghost.

"Take it off!" Glennon shouted.

"I can't." Kit's voice vibrated along the rope and straight through to Glennon's bones. It wiggled the fishhook in his chest, making all of the little muscles in his chest spasm.

Glennon hoisted himself to his feet and stalked toward Kit, trying to ignore the pain. "Get the ropes off us. You have *no* business haunting either me or my mom. And it wasn't funny to climb out of Christopher Picard's grave! That wasn't a funny joke."

"I'm not laughing." Kit's face, shrouded in darkness, showed no hint of an expression. His voice was flat and dead.

Kit dropped the portion of Glennon's rope that he held, and Glennon watched its end disappear into the grave beside him.

"Glennon," Lee said from behind him. "Glennon, I know a Kit at school. His real name is Christopher. *Kit* is a nickname for *Christopher*."

Glennon came to a halt. "*You're* Christopher Picard?"

"I am." Kit turned to the tombstone. "Lived well. Died terribly."

"1816! You *died* in 1816?"

"Sure did." The wind around Kit buzzed against the ground and swirled harder. "I told you. It was take your son to work day, though I suppose back then, sons always got taken to work. It wasn't like now, where everyone goes to school. I worked and I sailed, right along with my dad, and we both died. We *both* ended up here."

His dad? Glennon didn't bother to ask who Kit's dad was, because who else could he be? Who else had been with Kit from the beginning? "*Everett.*"

Everett wasn't in the glade, but then suddenly, there he stood. He wore his human form, and as they watched, he flickered. His blue eyes frosted over. The tips of his hair turned into curling icicles. His skin became translucent and clear. He was made entirely of ice.

"Dad!" protested Kit. "You don't need to be here. I can do this."

"Clearly, I do need to be here. Clearly, you cannot do this. If you could do this, you would have done this already." A blast of freezing air funneled out of Everett's icy body. Kit flinched away, backing toward the crumbling church.

"Why are you trying to hurt us?" Glennon shouted.

"I haven't been trying to hurt you." Everett's voice sounded the same as waves sliding over rocks, unearthly and strange. "I've been trying to *kill* you."

Glennon stumbled back a step, bumping into Lee who stood close behind him. Lee moved sideways so they both wouldn't tumble into a heap and stood at his shoulder.

"The island is very clear that it wants your lives, but that's been difficult to do, what with the three keepers protecting you inside Graving. But the island wants you dead, and it wants you dead by The Waning. Job and the keepers have refused to take your souls, so here I am, doing the work they should have done. Do you know what trouble you've been for me?" Everett said. "You and Job and the keepers and your stupid *cat*."

Everett lashed out at Lee. His hand darted through the air, his entire body moving too fast to track. Air *whoomphed* when he parted through it and grabbed the front of Lee's jacket. Lee's feet skidded across the ground as he dragged her toward the grave he'd climbed from.

"That stupid cat of yours. The island *hates* cats. Did you

know that? It hates cats. Do you know how many rats your cat has destroyed since being here?" Everett drew Lee closer to him.

Stop, Glennon wanted to say. All the muscles in his body locked in place. He watched the scene unfold before his eyes *and* inside his mind. Memory overlapped as it often did. Their dad grabbing Seamus and chucking him out of the house, complaining about the cat's fur. Lee yelling and running for Seamus, but their dad wrapping his hands around her upper arms. *Glennon watching, unable to stop their dad from being so cruel.*

He saw himself in the past, frozen and unable to help. But the part of himself that froze and forgot how to move wasn't helping him now. All it was doing was making Lee get hurt.

"Now is not then," he said out loud. He grabbed for Lee, but he forgot that he was holding the compact. The mirror slipped in his grip. He snatched for it and managed to grab it, but one of the two mirrors popped loose. It bounced against Everett's arm. Sudden, hissing heat filled the air; the ice of Everett's arm began to steam.

Everett's fingers spasmed open, and he dropped Lee. She scrambled to her feet, and she and Glennon bolted to the tree line.

Everett's slippery voice wound around the glade. He held his opposite hand over the watery wound that leaked from his upper arm. "You can't escape us."

Glennon and Lee hid behind a tree, tucking their bodies close together.

Everett's head fell toward one side, strange in the way it almost seemed to topple off his neck. "There's no way off the island. We've made sure of it. Isle Philippeaux wants you."

"But why?" Lee whispered.

Everett heard. He chuckled. The laughter swung on creaking hinges and rocked this way and that, until all of a sudden, it slammed shut, stopping altogether. "You are alive, and all things that are dead crave life. The island is hungry."

Glennon didn't understand. How could Isle Philippeaux be hungry? It was just an island!

"All we need is to get to Townsend's boat," Glennon whispered to Lee. "If we get her to the boat, we can leave."

"How do you not understand?" Everett said. In a burst of light and freezing air, he appeared before them, his face gaping and terrible, not a foot from their own "*There is no way off the island.*"

The ghosts vanished. Silence crawled through the graveyard. It stiffened the feel of the air around them and pressed Glennon's body toward the ground. The bumpy glade before them was filled with the dead grass and decaying leaves of winter, gray rough-hewn headstones, and no matter where Glennon looked, no evening light shone on the two ghosts.

"Where…where did they go?" Glennon peered around the graveyard.

"They're going to come back, aren't they?" Lee said, shivering inside her coat. "They're going to come back, and they're going to jump out and scream at us, aren't they?" Her mittened hands crept up and over her ears. Her body was in a slow descent, collapsing in on herself and turning her into something that *wasn't* her. She folded onto the ground with her knees tucked against her chest. "They want us to be scared, don't they?"

Glennon dug inside his coat pocket and found the pair of earplugs he'd taken to carrying around on Uncle Job's advice. Kneeling, he tugged Lee's hands away from her head.

"If they jump out and scream at us, these will help." Glennon stuck the purple plugs in her ears. "Tell me about monsters, Lee. Please. What's your favorite one?"

"I like banshees," Lee whispered. She pulled her puffy hood over her head and clasped her hands over her hood, covering her ears with three layers. She squished her eyes shut and buried her face against her knees. "Banshees are always women."

Glennon crept into the graveyard, holding the compact at an angle so he could see the reflection of his rope in the one remaining mirror. He had to find where the ropes disappeared, even if Kit and Everett were sure to come back. He had no choice; Mom would never wake if he didn't fix things.

"Banshees cry a lot." Lee's breath rasped as she filled her lungs deep. "I cry a lot too. Their eyes get red, like mine do."

Glennon tracked the ropes. His rope didn't lead to Kit's grave, but to the one right beside Christopher Picard's. Nothing but a blank tombstone sat at its head, reminding Glennon of when he'd stood beside Uncle Job and watched an invisible hand carve words in the rock with an invisible chisel. The end of his rope plunged straight into the heart of the unnamed grave beneath his feet.

Beside it, a second rope fell into another unmarked grave—*Mom's*. Fear cracked through him. *He was staring at his own grave.*

"Banshees keen," Lee said behind him—

A gale blasted through the graveyard and picked Glennon up by the armpits. He screamed, the sound scraping his throat raw. He struggled to free himself, but he was caught fast.

"I drowned in 1816, Glen." Everett's voice shot through the cemetery. "I drowned and my body became a drowned thing, turning into water and ice. I have lived on this isle for nearly two hundred years. *Two hundred years!* I will live here for a thousand more, and *you* will live with us too, Glen."

Glennon *hated* that name. His name *wasn't* Glen!

Lee's voice ran beneath Everett's, saying, "Keening is kind of like crying, except it's more than crying. It's weeping. Crying, along with wailing."

"On Superior, the dead always end up here. The island is a

vortex. It sucks everything and everyone into it." Everett's arms tangled around Glennon in the air. Jagged ice pricked against his coat and brought stinging tears to Glennon's eyes. "This is the only choice, Glen."

Glen, raged Glennon's dad inside his mind. This time, he couldn't stop the overlap of memory. *Glen,* his dad screamed. *Glen,* as if his dad were talking to a different person and not Glennon at all. *GLEN,* like his dad could scratch away Glennon's name and make him someone new…someone he liked and would be kind to.

You're supposed to be smart, Glen. You're supposed to be smart and obedient, Glen. You're supposed to be a good son, Glen. Glen, why aren't you a good son? At least Lee is smart. But what are you? Useless. Incompetent.

Fear ripped through Glennon. He struggled to think; his brain felt like wading through thick mud.

Worthless. Stupid.

Glennon didn't understand why his dad said such awful things—he didn't think it should be hard for someone to be kind to him. He didn't think he was useless or incompetent; he tried so hard to be good. He didn't think he should ever be told he was worthless or stupid, because he wasn't. *He wasn't.* He didn't think he should ever have to be called Glen.

"Banshees keen," said Lee from somewhere at the edge

of the field, from inside the cocoon of her coat. "They keen, because they know someone's going to die."

"As soon as Isle Philippeaux has what it needs, it will disappear. *You* are what it needs. Your life is what it needs," Everett said from somewhere very near to his ear. Heavy breathing puffed against his neck, each huff of air freezing the tender skin covering his jugular. "Do you understand, Glen?"

"That's not my name," he whispered.

"Do you understand that when Isle Philippeaux disappears, it will take you with it, whether or not you're dead first?" Everett said.

Sudden fiery desperation sung through Glennon. He kicked and fought against Everett's impossible icy body and the wind that held him fast and the memories that rocked through his brain.

"That means—it means that banshees predict death," Lee said.

"The island needs life to exist," Everett said.

"Banshees foretell death," said Lee.

"The island needs *your* life." Everett's voice scraped against the soft innards of Glennon's ears.

"Banshees *herald death!*" shouted Lee.

"Isle Philippeaux needs you to die, Glen!"

Glen. Glennnn, GLEN! his dad raged in the back of Glennon's mind.

Everett shoved Glennon toward the grave the island had dug for him. The earth yawned open, hunger and need foaming out of the ground to grab at Glennon. Deep shadows scuttled over the edges of Glennon's vision, the sides of the grave stretching around him. He kicked and shouted, "My name *isn't* Glen."

Lee shouted too, her voice drowning out their dad's inside Glennon's mind, *"BANSHEES ARE HARBINGERS OF DOOM!"*

And Glennon, using every ounce of life inside him, gripped the broken compact tight in his hand. He pressed it to his chest, to the place where the fishing hook speared through his bones. Just like when the mirror had fallen against Everett, smoke filled the air. The rope lit on fire and burned.

Everett gagged on the smoke. He thrust back from Glennon.

Glennon fell, his shoulder and hip ramming into the ground and one leg dangling into the open grave. The silver fishing hook fell out of his chest, and immediately, the pain in his ribs disappeared. He rolled to his feet, tripping over the uneven ground in the darkness and away from the open grave. Graving Lighthouse, not far from where they stood, swung its heavy, bright light across the sky. He bolted toward it, running straight at his sister, who'd gotten to her feet.

She pointed one finger in Everett's direction. "I am your

harbinger of doom! *You cannot take my brother!*" She drew her arm back and chucked her silver flashlight straight at the ghost.

Glennon glanced back.

Everett tried to twist away, but he didn't move fast enough. The flashlight hurtled straight into the place where his heart would have been, had he been alive and human. The end of it—the light facing outward—smacked him dead center, sticking into the ice of his torso. Scorching black smoke filled the air.

25

Glennon pelted through the woods. In one hand he held their last flashlight, and in the other he held the still smoking mirror, grateful he'd worn mittens. He swerved around a tree, and Lee swerved right behind him. The trees creaked and groaned. Branches twitched toward him. Roots rolled up beneath the ground and heaved in their direction.

The sense of *watchfulness* that always rose when the dead rats came around fell over Glennon, an ancient thing beneath the forest bed seeming to wake and tug at all the pieces of the island. This was not the ghosts. It was something else entirely.

Beating wings and a thick body swooped through the air. Instinctively, Glennon ducked and the creature flew past. He glanced at it and nearly ran into a tree. A bird sat on a branch, though it was devoid of feathers. Only white bones held it together. *Faster,* screamed the thing inside Glennon that was more animal than human.

They flew out of the woods and onto the gravel road that

led to Graving. They were almost there; they'd almost reached the light—

Kit burst into existence in front of them. He wore his human body, *not* his ghost form.

Glennon skidded to a halt. Lee rammed into his back—she was following so close!—and they both collapsed in a heap, with Glennon on his knees and Lee laying half over his feet.

"Why are you doing this?" Glennon said. "I thought we were friends."

"We *are* friends!" Kit's eyes grew wide, all of the sadness Glennon had once felt in the graveyard filling his face. "We could always be friends. We'd be best friends if you stayed."

"I don't want to stay here. I want to go home. I want to be alive."

"*Me too!*" Kit's shout strained the air, and Glennon winced against the feel of it. "I want to be alive too! But I don't have a choice. The island doesn't give us a choice. I didn't have a choice when I died!"

A massive weight filled Glennon. Kit was just as stuck on this island as they were, the major difference being that he was dead.

"I didn't have a choice when my dad's ship crashed. When he drowned in the water. When I crawled up on this horrible island and thought I'd been saved. I didn't have a choice when The Waning came—when the island disappeared, when it sucked my life straight out of me. I didn't have a choice when it stole every ounce of myself until I had nothing left, until I *died!*"

Wind kicked up around Kit, blowing down the gravel road. It struck Glennon. It pressed against his mouth and for a moment, he felt as if he were drowning, as if little clawed fingers had scraped down his throat and plugged up his lungs.

"I've been stuck here for nearly two hundred years with my dad! I had *no choice!*" The wind spooling off Kit disappeared, and Glennon gasped in a breath.

"What's The Waning, Kit?" Glennon asked, when he could breathe. He was desperate to avoid Kit's existence. He couldn't imagine the awfulness of it, of being stuck on an island for so many years with Everett. It's not like Everett was nice to Kit...or anyone, for that matter.

Kit's human form began to fade away, and his blurred ghost form took over, hurting Glennon's eyes. His curled lips peeled back, revealing the darkness of the bottom of Lake Superior inside his mouth. "The Waning is why I look like *this.* Anyone who dies during The Waning looks like this. The Waning is when life will be sucked from anyone who's still alive on the isle. The Waning is when it disappears. The waning is when your life will funnel straight out of your body and into the island."

That was how Glennon's family would die if they stayed on Isle Philippeaux.

"We met here once." Kit pointed at the gravel at his feet and the bend in the road. "You biked straight through me. The island wanted me to take your soul then, because your Uncle Job and the keepers kept refusing. They kept protecting you, kept begging the island not to kill you. I was supposed to tie you to the rope and drag you into the grave. I stuck the hook into you, and I thought I'd caught you...but then your cat, your *stupid* cat—"

"My cat's *not* stupid...and you sounded just like your dad when you said that." Glennon climbed to his feet, drew back his arm, and threw the flashlight he'd clutched tight while they'd run. He was tired of listening to Kit make excuses. He had no more time to waste.

The flashlight hit Kit in the middle. He staggered as if Glennon had punched him. A bit of his human form flickered back into view, and Glennon saw the horror and sadness and anger that etched into his face. Glennon ignored the pang of sympathy that ran through him and took off, veering around the ghost with Lee following close behind.

They ran around the curve in the road and there, before them, rose Graving Lighthouse with its white light swooping across the sky.

They ran straight up the front steps of the Third Keeper's

house where Uncle Job stood in the doorway. He held the door open and stared over their heads into the darkness of the woods.

In the doorway, standing beneath Uncle Job's arm, Glennon turned back to Kit.

The skeleton bird flew out of the woods and landed on Kit's shoulder. Kit flinched, pain ribboning through his eyes. He shouted, "You can try to outrun me, but you'll never outrun the island. *There's no way to leave!*" His voice shifted. It was two-toned, both high and low at the same time. voice. It was almost as though Isle Philippeaux itself spoke through him, as if the island had possessed him.

He flew up the stairs then, racing after Lee. Behind him, Uncle Job slammed the door.

"Mom!" Glennon ran into Mom's room. "Mom, there are ghosts! And they want to kill us! And they... Mom?"

Mom still slept. Seamus curled over her chest, right near her throat, his massive head tucked beneath her chin. Glennon held out the mirror and without thinking twice, pressed it into their mom's chest. Black smoke curled into the air.

"Mirrors show the truth of things," Glennon said, repeating Keeper Sanz's words.

"Mirrors show the state of the soul," said Uncle Job from where he stood in the doorway.

Mom's hands moved beneath the quilt and reached for

Seamus. Without opening her eyes, she said, "Why are you burning things in my bedroom?"

"We're not burning things, Mom," Glennon said. "It's ghosts!"

"Glennon, don't make things up. You know that's a terrible thing to do," she said.

Glennon shriveled beneath her words. How was he supposed to convince her?

"It's the ghost world, Ruby," Uncle Job said.

"*Job.*" Mom sighed.

"*Ruby.*" Uncle Job sighed right back. "Your kids have been racing across this island, getting chased by ghosts and who knows what else. I know you know something's wrong here, and this is it. This is what's wrong. This island is an island of ghosts, and I'm one of them. Isn't it enough that you keep your children cooped up in your house with that husband of yours? Why keep them here as well—"

Mom's eyes flew open and seemed to swallow up the dim light of the room. "Don't you dare judge me, Job."

"And now, you're refusing to look at the truth of this place!"

Lee began to slowly tiptoe out of the room. Glennon backed away as well, not liking the itch that spread across his skin. He *hated* standing in the middle of adults arguing.

"Job, I'm *tired*," Mom said.

"You've slept the entire day away," Uncle Job said.

Mom laughed. "I have not. I only laid down a little bit ago. Everett stopped by and he ate dinner with me, since none of you were around. We ate, and I was so tired afterward that I came to bed."

Silence fell through the room. It crackled and popped, the kind of silence that made Glennon feel horribly sick. He said, "Mom, Everett wasn't here. No one's had dinner."

"*I* had dinner. With Everett. We sat in the living room in front of the fire." Mom's face creased, confusion knitting her brows together.

"You slept all day, Mom. You haven't gotten out of bed," Lee said. "You must've had a dream."

"She was being haunted," Uncle Job said.

Glennon spun to Uncle Job. "You didn't know? Shouldn't you have been able to stop him?"

Uncle Job lifted both shoulders. "I've only been dead half a year. I'm not as experienced a ghost as Everett."

"Enough. Stop!" Mom sliced both hands through the air, severing their conversation in half. "Everett is not a ghost. *You're* not a ghost! I'm not being haunted!"

"How many times have you seen Everett?" Glennon asked, thinking about how many times he'd seen Kit without Lee also seeing him.

"He had coffee here the other morning," Mom said. "Right after the shipwreck."

Lee shook her head. Glennon shook his also.

"We had coffee. We all ate together."

"No," Uncle Job said.

"I don't understand."

"Mom. You've been getting sicker. You slept all day. We've never seen Everett here, except for the night of the shipwreck." Glennon reached out to her, but then let his arm drop. It all was so confusing.

Lee said, "Glennon kept seeing Kit too when no one else saw him. Glennon said he stayed the night here and that he listened to the ghost story Townsend told, but I never saw him. Kit was haunting Glennon. Everett was haunting *you*."

"Leeunah, you're telling stories," Mom said.

Lee's hands fisted at her sides. "I'm *not*!"

"She's not, Mom. It's the truth. We were both haunted. Lee wasn't, though, because she always had Seamus, and Seamus protected her. You had a fishing hook stuck into you. It had a rope at the end, and the rope led to a grave, and the rope made you tired and was probably trying to suck out your life! I had one inside me too. It made my chest hurt really bad, right in the middle." Glennon's words flowed fast enough that his mouth tripped over them. He touched his chest, right in the middle, on the bone that connected the two sides of his ribcage.

Mom's hand floated up to her own sternum. Her eyes widened, and she murmured, "I've been hurting too. The pain is gone though."

"That's because we destroyed the rope!" Lee said.

Mom said, "How am I supposed to believe any of this? How am I supposed to believe that you're dead, Job? Dead means gone, and you're right here."

Glennon didn't have any more mirrors left to make Uncle Job shift forms. Both sides of the silver compact had been charred by the fight with Everett and by destroying his and Mom's ropes. Desperate, he said, "I don't know how to convince you." If he couldn't convince her, he wouldn't be able to get her to leave the island.

Uncle Job held up one large hand to Glennon. The motion said *stop*. "It's not your job to convince adults, Glennon. Adults are the ones who should protect you, not the other way around."

And in the same way that Everett and Kit had transformed without Glennon using a mirror, Uncle Job transformed as well. His human form faded away, until all that stood before them was a dripping wet, partly translucent tree.

26

Glennon had seen this once. It'd been a terrible, confusing moment.
He'd stood beside Uncle Job as they'd looked over the edge of
Graving's cliff and down at the *Anabeth* as she'd drowned beneath
Superior's heavy waves. Mist had swirled around Uncle Job, and
for the smallest of moments, he'd appeared as a tree, with water-
logged branches and his head made up of a mass of knots.

Glennon hadn't been imagining things. All along, he'd
been right. All along, he should have believed himself.

Mom gasped. Her hand flew to her mouth.

"Whoa," Lee said.

"Ghosts haunt this island, Ruby." Uncle Job's voice creaked
and groaned, just like the trees outside in the woods. "If we
haunted a house, we'd inhabit the house; we'd live in the walls
and in the floors. But here, we live in the island. We live *because
of* the island."

"What is this?" Mom said, her voice low and furious.
"What's happening? Is this a joke? This is a terrible joke."

"*Ruby.*" Uncle Job stretched out his limbs. "Our ghost forms show the shape of our souls, and our souls are mangled by the moment of our death. I was killed by a tree falling mid-storm."

This was why Kit looked like an absence of energy, why Everett was frozen, why Townsend looked drowned, why Miss Lacey had lightening—she must have been electrocuted.

"For the island to exist, it needs to consume life, *human* life. It only appears when it's running out of energy. For the past months, it's turned visible, so it could lure ships and people onto it to be killed. It lured you. But it will disappear for good soon, and when it does, you'll disappear as well."

"I don't understand," Mom whispered.

"We're going to die!" Glennon shouted.

Lee appeared in the doorway. She must've walked away for a moment, because when she came in, she held up the First Keeper's atlas. "The island is a sort of ghost too. Maybe every time it turns visible, it's slightly different. Maybe that's why there are so many versions of the map of Isle Philippeaux."

Uncle Job took the atlas and opened it to the middle. He handed it to Mom and pointed to small numbers at the very top that Glennon hadn't noticed. *1744.* "Miss Lacey in the library told me about this map. This is from a map drawn by Jacques-Nicolas Bellin. It was the first time Isle Philippeaux was ever drawn, because it was the first time someone living managed to escape."

That meant escape was possible!

Mom closed the atlas and pressed her fingertips to the front cover. "Everett was never here? You three are sure of it?"

"We wouldn't lie," Lee said.

"I knew something was wrong with Everett. I just didn't know what." She faced the window and peered out into the darkness of Superior. "I always trust my gut when it tells me someone is dangerous, but I didn't with Everett. It's just like with Hurley."

It took Glennon a moment to realize Mom had changed the subject, slightly. She no longer talked about Everett, but instead about his dad.

"It's *exactly* like with Hurley, Job! Why do I not trust myself?" Mom walked toward Uncle Job.

"It's hard to always trust yourself. It's even harder to know what to do with the information your gut provides you," Uncle Job said.

Quietly, Mom said, "Job, Hurley has asked me so many times how I would survive without him. So many times. When he's mad at me. When I've made a mistake. When I accidentally take a wrong turn while driving. And do you know what I think every time he asks me?"

Uncle Job waited, his hands hanging loose at his sides. He no longer wore his ghost form. Glennon looked at Lee to see that tears snaked down her cheeks.

"*Easily.* Every time he asks how I would ever manage to survive without him, I think, *I would survive without you so very easily.*" Mom's serene mask dropped away, leaving behind sadness and pain that made the bottoms of Glennon's lungs ache. "But every time he left, I ran to other people, because I couldn't stand being alone. I got your letter and decided that coming here was a better choice than staying in that house. At least here, with you, I could be safe."

Protect Mom; keep her safe; help her! Those are the things Glennon had always wanted to do, and yet, he'd never been able to. He hadn't been able to protect her from Isle Philippeaux… and he hadn't been able to protect her from his dad.

Glennon licked his lips. Tasting salt, he rubbed his eyes, wetting his jacket sleeve with his own hurt.

Uncle Job cried too, a soft sort of crying. The tears themselves held traces of deep blue, as if the depths of Superior leaked from inside him.

"If you're telling me we need to leave, then I believe you," Mom said, brisk and final. Her mask fell back in place, hiding away the pain. "Although this ghost nonsense is all a bit confusing."

"You need to leave tonight," Uncle Job added.

"*Tonight?*"

"The Waning will happen at midnight."

A harsh knock sounded at the front door. Confusion knit Uncle Job's brow. He left the room and headed down the stairs. On the other side of the door, Keeper Orwell stood. He held aloft an ancient lantern.

"The weather's changing," the First Keeper said.

Glennon, who had always paid close attention to voices and the swift, small ways they could change, heard not the First Keeper, but the two-toned pitch that had lived inside Kit's voice when he'd stood on the gravel road and shouted at them. He heard *the island*.

Uncle Job peered outside, toward the sky that was cut in half by the swooping light of Graving, and said, "Isle Philippeaux will make one last attempt at drowning ships."

Something warred inside of Uncle Job. He glanced back at his family who stood on the stairs, then back at the First Keeper and said, "I have to do my job."

"Job!" Mom said.

"I'm sorry." Uncle Job stepped into the evening. "This job was given to me by the island. There is only so much I can do to resist what it asks of me."

And Glennon knew that however they would get off Isle Philippeaux, they would have to do it alone.

27

"Don't go," Glennon said, and Uncle Job paused before disappearing entirely into the dark. Mist whisked off Uncle Job's shoulders. His eyes were wide and black, pupils dilated.

"Don't leave us, Job," Mom said. "Not now. We need your help."

"We all need to get off the island," Lee said.

"*You* need to get off the island. I'm stuck here, but you are not. You have a choice in this," Uncle Job said, "but I will exist on this island forever. I'm not free from it. I can't go entirely against its wishes. I *can't*. I don't know what the consequences would be."

Consequences? Glennon knew what consequences were like. There had always been consequences for going against his dad or asking him to stop. Stop yelling, stop calling them names, stop being angry all the time. In so many ways, it was easier to stand still and let his dad's rage pass. It was what their family did: they existed while their dad raged, and existing made it possible to survive until later. Maybe Uncle Job was just existing right now, waiting for someone's—the island's—rage to pass.

Uncle Job twined his fingers over the edge of the door and slowly pushed it closed, eyes like black holes watching them until it snapped shut.

"The Waning will happen at midnight when the date changes to the twenty-first," said Glennon, still facing the closed door. The house felt empty without Uncle Job in it. "Isle Philippeaux will disappear tonight."

"We need to leave, even if Uncle Job isn't helping us," Lee said. "We need to pack."

"I'm already packed," Mom said, still staring at the door. "I've always—I'm always packed."

Lee pushed at Glennon. They both ran up the stairs. The first thing he grabbed were the papers beneath his bed, though he left behind the writing he'd made for his dad. It wasn't something he needed. Then he scrounged for every shiny object inside the house, questioning the shine of the outside of a lantern, the shine of the back of a metal spoon that had gotten tossed among the plasticware, the shine of the small, rectangular mirror he found inside Lee's caboodle that housed makeup and stickers, the shine of the buckle of a belt, even the shine of the glass that covered over a small picture of their family. He loaded everything that was reflective into his own backpack.

What else could he pack that would affect the ghosts?

"Cats," he said and went to find Seamus.

He found him holding sentry at the bottom of the staircase, glaring at the front door through which Uncle Job had disappeared.

Steps sounded in the hallway above, and Glennon found Mom carrying a suitcase and buttoning up the sequin coat his dad had tried to toss out.

"Battle garments." Mom wore the jacket over a pair of jeans, and she'd layered lipstick over her mouth, a purple that matched the pomegranates she liked to buy at holidays.

"Makeup isn't a battle garment," Glennon said.

Mom's smile trembled. The purple shone against her white teeth. "Pretty clothes and makeup can be armor just as much as chain mail. It all depends on who and what you're fighting."

Glennon couldn't argue—he had no idea what would stop the ghosts or what would free them from the isle. If Mom thought lipstick would help, who was he to say?

At the bottom of the stairs, Mom took out her winter coat and buttoned it over the sequin jacket. Outside, the winds continued to rise. Glennon thought of Uncle Job and the keepers as they'd stood in the middle of the storm that had destroyed the *Anabeth* so many days ago. Of Townsend and Kit standing by the lake while dark clouds covered the sky. Of

Miss Lacey and the lightning that had split from the back of her hand.

"*Oh*," Glennon said aloud, realizing what he hadn't considered before.

Was it possible the ghosts *caused* the storms?

He looked up to find both Mom and Lee staring at him. "I think the ghosts make the storms happen."

"Why?" Mom asked.

"To kill people," Glennon said. "Everett told us that. He wanted to kill us, so that our life would drain into Isle Philippeaux."

Lee added, "Ghosts don't have life of their own. They have to take another's life to keep existing. So they cause the storms to wreck ships. People die, and they suck away their lives."

"Just like in Townsend's ghost story. '*I hear the dead. They need life. They starve!*'" Glennon said, repeating Townsend's words. All along, it hadn't been a story at all. It'd been the truth. "Uncle Job said it too. He said he feels deep hunger, though he wouldn't tell us what he was hungry for."

"The ghosts are hungry for life," Lee said. She strapped on her backpack and Glennon picked up Seamus, tucking his long legs and massively fluffy body inside. She stuffed beside him her moon boots, choosing to wear tennis shoes instead, probably so she could run faster.

Mom threw open the door. Outside, the temperature had

dropped farther. The thermometer read eleven degrees. Wind buffeted against them and pushed their shoulders and grasped the warm air from their lungs.

Glennon ducked his head and shoved his way toward the car. "Job!" Mom yelled.

Glennon paused, one hand on the car's back door. To his right, he could see the outline of a large figure standing beside Graving Lighthouse. It held a lantern high, the light inside swinging and flickering. It illuminated Uncle Job's frazzled beard.

"I know you are stuck here," Mom yelled louder, "but we aren't. Help us, please!"

Glennon had no idea how Uncle Job could hear her from so far away, especially against the wind, but his uncle stayed where he was, listening. Glennon opened the car door and slid inside, his eyes watering from the cold. Lee took her normal spot beside Mom.

"Where to?" Mom asked, voice wobbling. She cleared her throat and started the car.

"Townsend's," Glennon said.

He'd thought of using her boat before. He'd never imagined, though, that it would be the only option for getting off the island.

He understood now that Townsend had never been a monster. She hadn't attacked him, like Miss Lacey. She hadn't tried to hurt him, like Everett. She hadn't tried to convince him to join them, like Kit.

She had helped him once before, and he hoped she would help again.

28

"*Are you sure we can't stay until the storm passes?*" *Mom drove* slowly and carefully down the gravel road, and though the speed made Glennon more than a little antsy, he knew it was safe, especially with the growing storm.

"Either we take a boat in the middle of a storm, or we stay and get eaten by the island," Glennon said.

They reached Ingram Lighthouse faster than when they'd biked, and though harsh winds raged around them, the island didn't play tricks with the road like it had when Glennon had biked alone.

Mom parked the car, and they ran for the Lighthouse. They pounded on the door, all shouting to be let in. After the longest ten seconds of Glennon's life, the door opened to reveal Townsend standing with both hands on her hips and her black coat covering her head. Warmth and the scent of bread poured out from the door. She said, "The entire isle heard about your fight with Everett."

Horribly, sickeningly, Glennon realized it was possible that she wouldn't let them in. She might not help them. It was probably too risky for her too. She lived here, just like Uncle Job. If she helped, would the island retaliate somehow? What would the consequences be?

"Nobody wants to fight, Everett," said a voice from the kitchen.

Townsend dropped her arms and stood back, allowing them entry, though she did so with a glare.

"We need help," Glennon said.

"Let them in, Townsend," said the voice. It turned out to be Keeper Delmont. He stood at the kitchen sink and peered out an open window. "Nobody wants to fight Everett, and yet, many of us end up doing so."

From over by the oven range, Mr. Traxler said, "We do, and we fail, because we aren't strong enough to contend with the island. It pours energy and life into Everett. It gives him extra strength. And so here we find ourselves stuck, baking bread and watching out the window for the ships and their passengers who may join us." But he said all this cheerfully, while pulling a loaf out of the oven. "Banana bread!"

Townsend slumped into a chair.

Her dad lay the bread on a cooling rack on the table. Cutting slices, he set them out on delicate plates inlaid with gold leaves along their edges, then slathered cream cheese over a piece and slid it across the table toward Glennon's mom.

"Dad!" Townsend said, no longer slumping.

"*Townsend.*" He passed another plate to Lee and a third to Glennon. "We help those in need. We protect those who need protection. We feed those who are hungry."

"We can hardly protect ourselves, much less anyone else," Townsend muttered.

"You're protecting me just fine," said a third male's voice.

Glennon turned to find Gibraltar sitting on a twin bed in one of the rooms.

"Are you a ghost too?" asked Glennon.

"No. Not for lack of the island trying to kill me though." He folded and unfolded his hands, which lay in his lap.

"You're giving up?" Glennon asked. "Have you stopped trying to find a way to escape?"

A grin crept over his mouth. "*Never.* I have no aims of becoming a ghost."

Townsend slid back down in her chair, nearly slipping straight under the table. Even grumpier than before, she said, "He bedazzled my boat."

"What?" Glennon asked.

"He bedazzled my boat!" Popping back up, she threw her arms in the air. "With sea glass and aluminum foil!"

"No boats exist here that would ward off ghosts, so I made one of my own." Gibraltar's smile slipped away. "Though I need a ghost to pilot the boat. I need their help to make it through the storm."

"We've already apologized," Keeper Delmont said, still looking outside. "We've no desire to engage in direct battle against the island. There's no way we would win." He backed away from the window. "It's coming. I see their lights."

"Everett?" Glennon asked, voice cracking halfway through. He cleared his throat and didn't attempt the word again. He was too nervous.

"Worse," said Keeper Delmont. "A ship."

"A *ghost* ship?" Lee asked.

"*Worse.*" Keeper Delmont turned toward them, revealing his face for the first time.

Mom gasped, then flinched away, fumbling with her plate. Keeper Delmont's throat gaped open, right beneath his jaw, looking as if he wore two mouths instead of one. From the puckering skin came whispering fingers of white smoke. A steady stream of fog enveloped the contours of his face, ghosting over the brown of his eyes. It looked like a knife wound, one that had never...would never heal. It must have been how he'd died.

He said, "It's a ship of the living."

29

Keeper Delmont unlatched the back door. Wind whipped through the opening, snatching the handle from his grasp and sending it flying. He stood in the tumult, one hand raised as if to greet the ship.

In the warmth of the kitchen, Glennon had, for a moment, forgotten the cold outside. Forgotten the impending storm. Forgotten the black, depthless night.

"They'll be here soon. In minutes," Keeper Delmont said.

"Are they going to land?" Glennon asked.

Everyone in the kitchen turned to him, including Keeper Delmont and his face that split wide with holes.

"They're going to *crash*," Townsend said. "They'll run aground. The ship will sink. If anyone survives the wreck and makes it to the island, then they'll get the life sucked straight out of them when The Waning happens at midnight. People will die."

In the distance, lights bobbed and twisted on the dark lake, turning into fireflies that danced across the waves.

"And you're all just going to sit here and do nothing?" Glennon remembered saying, *That's all you're going to do? Those sailors will die!* to the three keepers at Graving, and Keeper Orwell saying, *Ships wreck*, as if it were an everyday occurrence.

"What do you want us to do?" Townsend said. "There's nothing we *can* do!"

"Oh, you could do something," Gibraltar said. "You could go out and save them. You could turn their ship away!"

Townsend shoved up from the table. She pointed hard at the door and the ship. Her black hood inched away from her forehead, revealing her hairline and the rope fibers that threaded along her scalp. "Helping them would *hurt us!*"

"You're ghosts!" Glennon said.

"And that means my existence doesn't matter?"

Furious, Glennon flipped up his own hood and zipped his coat all the way to his chin. He walked out the back of Ingram Lighthouse and onto the beach. Bright light flooded from Ingram's tower. It beamed out and over the lake.

"Lovely ship, isn't it?"

Glennon nearly jumped out of his skin. He skidded on the wet rocks, trying to catch his footing. The voice beside him wasn't Lee's or Townsend's, Mom's or Gibraltar's, Mr. Traxler's or Keeper Delmont's. It was Everett's; it was the voice of water crashing and lapping against the shore. And beneath that was another pitch: the voice of the phantom island—Isle Philippeaux.

Everett was standing beside him, his thumbs hooked around overalls that connected to a pair of rubber slickers. Besides that, he wore nothing. No shirt against the cold. No hat to warm his ears. He looked human, even though no human would be able to stand in these temperatures without shivering. When he glanced away from the ship and toward Glennon, his eyes took on the shine of frosted ice.

"I stood on that ship for a while tonight. I stood on her prow. I became her figurehead. I learned the names of her crew," Everett said. "I met those who will soon join me on this island."

Glennon tried to tiptoe away from the ghost...and the rope Everett held in one hand.

"You will join me as well. Isle Philippeaux would be delighted to give you a watery grave, just as much as an earthly grave on the island, Glen. You could even have both!"

"Leave my son alone," Mom said from behind Glennon. She was small and puffy in her winter clothes, wrapped tight in her long quilted jacket, the length of it covering her to the tops of her knees.

"Mom, stay away!" Glennon tried to climb across the rocks to stand between Everett and her, but he skidded against the wet surface and slipped. Falling, he banged his knee against a stone.

"You can have a grave as well," Everett said to Mom. "I already tried to give you one."

Mom stared Everett down, her calm mask in place, the one Glennon had watched fall over her eyes so many times before. It had always frustrated him, hadn't it? The way Mom didn't seem to feel things. He knew that wasn't the truth though. The mask she wore was how she protected herself, and right now, she was using it to protect *him*.

"What sort of grave would you like? I'm not beyond being considerate and letting you choose," Everett said.

"I am not scared of you. I have known monsters," Mom said.

"You haven't known me," Everett said, not bothering to deny his monstrousness.

"*I have known monsters.*" Her calm body didn't flinch as the wind rose around them, whirling in a small funnel around both her and Everett.

Glennon crouched on the ground, the wet rocks dampening his jeans. He ducked his head against the furious wind.

"It's difficult to be a ghost, isn't it? It's hard to be a monster." Mom's mittened hand wrapped around the zipper to her jacket and the other around the top of her coat, as if they needed something to hold tight to. "You hurt others, when truly, you are what hurts. You hurt others *because* you hurt. It's difficult to hurt."

Everett's skin had begun to take on a frozen sheen. In the

light that poured from Ingram, the ice of his ghost form took on the whirling pattern of a flower or a snowflake. "I already told your son. I'm not trying to hurt you."

"You're just trying to kill us?"

"I have to give your life to the island. It's my job. I have no choice."

The ghosts kept saying that, that they had no choice, that the consequences would be too terrible if they went against Isle Philippeaux. Was it true? Or was it just a lie they tried to convince themselves was real? Glennon picked himself up from the rocks.

"But in the process of killing us, you hurt us," Mom said. "You cannot escape your hurt, and so you hurt others. You take out your revenge on the living because you cannot take out your revenge on the island. You cannot escape, and so you drag others to join you. Misery loves company."

"I don't have a choice!" Everett roared, sudden and loud and shocking to Glennon's eardrums. Everett's mouth gaped open, icy jaw unhinging like a snake, coming free from his skull, and looking for all the world like it could swallow them whole.

Unfazed, Mom pointed at the ship in the distance. "Right now, you either spend time trying to capture us or *them,* and we are not nearly the life equal to the life that exists on that ship."

Everett wavered, turning to look back at the ship that bobbed closer to the coastline.

"Their ship might wrest free of this storm. You are not there to ensure success. Imagine if they escape with their lives intact. Imagine how angry the island will be then. I know you do not want to experience its wrath." Mom held out one hand toward Everett, saying, "And we will still be here. There's no way for us to escape."

Everett considered Mom, but then in a blink, he disappeared. Immediately, the gales of December that twisted around them vanished as well. Glennon coughed against the sudden easy breath that flooded his lungs. He grabbed at Mom whose shoulders drooped and spine bent, all the strength that had been present a moment before fading away.

"I sent Everett to that ship," Mom said.

"No." Glennon helped her toward Ingram. "No. You saved us."

"I traded our lives for theirs."

"We'll find a way to save them too." Glennon faced Ingram's doorway and spoke to the collection of ghosts and the living who stood there. "We're going to save them, aren't we? If we turn off Ingram's light, they won't be drawn here anymore, right?"

His gaze swept up to the top of the lighthouse. He watched the fixed light as it beamed into the night, flashing its *on-off, on-off, on-on-off* pattern. He crooked his head, feeling as if he stood before Graving instead of Ingram. He knew the rhythm of Graving's light well. *On-off, on-off, on-on-off.* Weren't the identification signals of lighthouses supposed to be different, so sailors could determine their location around an island?

As he watched the light, he felt the same pull he'd always felt at Graving. The light felt safe. It felt like home.

"Siren song," Glennon murmured. He found Townsend standing dead center of the door. "That's what it is, isn't it? It's like the ghost story you told. The light is like sirens who sing to sailors, and then the sailors crash their ships and die."

Townsend's whole body seemed to collapse beneath her black coat, just like Mom's had after Everett disappeared.

"We have to turn off the light," he said. "If we stop it, maybe the ship won't sail toward the isle."

"Our job is to keep the light on and keep it running," Townsend said. "We can't stop it."

"You might not be able to," Glennon said, "but we can."

30

Glennon left Mom at the door and raced into Ingram. He zoomed past the ghosts, but as he ran past Townsend, she grabbed her hood and yanked it back. Wind blasted through the room, shoving everyone back, including Glennon who smacked straight into a cupboard.

"You can't touch the light!" she roared, fear running through her voice.

Glennon roared too, with every inch of air inside his lungs, "You help those in need. You protect those who need protection!" He pointed at the banana bread and cream cheese on the table. "You feed those who are hungry!"

Townsend recoiled, and in that small window of time, Glennon flew through the kitchen and to the metal staircase.

On the second floor, Ingram's eye was open and set to blinking, *on-off, on-off, on-on-off.*

How was he supposed to break it? He hadn't bothered to carry anything up the stairs, and he had no idea how to turn off the light. Was there an off switch? How did you unscrew a lightbulb that was made up of dozens of thick glass panels half the size of your own body?

"Here," someone said from behind him, handing him a long, heavy piece of wood. He took it without looking and swung. It smashed into the light, and glass exploded every which way. He raised his arms to cover his face. A blast of air filled the room and a black coat blocked the shards from piercing him.

Tinkling glass fell on the metal floor. Glennon stayed huddled in Townsend's shadow. He looked at the piece of wood he held and recognized it as the wood of an oar from a boat. It was broken at both ends. Twice now, Townsend had been scared of helping him, but had done so anyway.

"Townsend?" Glennon asked, handing her the oar.

"Please don't." She took the wood and fixed it back beneath her tattered coat, hooking it into her shoulder joint. Her water-logged hand appeared at its other end.

"You could've stopped me. You could've not handed me your arm." He grinned suddenly, laughing. "Townsend, you literally gave me your arm!"

Giggling, she pulled up her hood and covered her drowned face. "The one good thing about being a ghost, I guess."

Glennon laughed again, but then stopped when her giggles died away. "Why did you help me?"

"I know what it's like to end up here and feel lost and confused. I wish someone would've helped me figure out how to escape." She hugged her now human looking arms around her body. "Isle Philippeaux is going to be so mad that I helped destroy the light, but…We help those in need. We protect those who need protection."

Glennon wanted to say something comforting to Townsend, but he didn't quite know what that was. Instead, he said, "We should collect the glass, can't let it go to waste! It's shiny."

Townsend picked up a flat shard of glass that hadn't broken into smithereens. In its reflection, her body shifted to her ghost form, though she didn't particularly seem to mind. She headed down the stairs, and Glennon's mom came up holding a small canvas sack.

Together, they began collecting the larger pieces of broken glass. He didn't know how they were supposed to keep the dead from winning. They'd broken only one light of many. There was no possible way to destroy all of the lights tonight, not unless *all* the ghosts agreed to help, and he didn't see that happening.

It would be impossible for them stop the isle completely, wouldn't it? All they could do was escape.

Back on the first floor, Glennon found everyone in the house hovering beside the door. Lee stood beside Gibraltar, who now was dressed in a rain jacket over winter clothing. Keeper Delmont and Mr. Traxler and Townsend were there as well, and they all wore their ghost forms.

Each of them was made of the way they'd died—just like Uncle Job had said. Townsend with her gray, wrinkly skin and oars for arms who must've drowned in the lake. Mr. Traxler who was made of ice, like Everett, who must've frozen to death. Keeper Delmont with his slit open throat, who must've died at the mercy of pirates.

The living and the dead stood together.

Glennon joined them, and then he headed straight out the door and into the storm, ready to face whatever would come next.

31

Shiny stones and bits of glass and patches of tinfoil were glued along the interior of Townsend's boat.

"I thought to stick them to the outsides as well," said Gibraltar, "but I knew if I did, the boat would track oddly in the water. Figured it was a better bet for us to be able to sail correctly and have the shiny bits on the inside. If they get close to us, they'll see their reflections. Ghosts don't like seeing the truth of what they are."

None of the ghosts responded, and Glennon noticed they took care not to glance inside the boat, all except for Townsend who seemed comfortable enough in her ghost form. She gestured for them to enter. There were only three seats, so while Mom and Lee sat on the front small bench, Glennon sat beside Gibraltar in the middle, and Townsend took her position by the motor. They all grabbed one shard of glass from the light to hold as protection.

"Look." Gibraltar pointed.

Glennon followed the line his finger made through the dark and found, in the distance, the steadily disappearing lights of the ship that had approached Isle Philippeaux. It must've turned away once Ingram had broken.

Townsend's boat slipped into the water, moving only because the ghosts helped propel them through the waves. Keeper Delmont and Mr. Traxler walked atop the water beside them, or...they *hovered* atop the water. Waves splashed against them, but the ghosts sliced straight through, not balking at the cold and wet. Glennon shuddered, turning his gaze from the place where Keeper Delmont's feet turned to mist and the black space between Mr. Traxler's shoes and Lake Superior.

All of a sudden, Townsend's boat ground to a halt, something catching against the hull.

"There's something beneath us," Glennon gasped. In front of him, Lee picked her feet off the bottom of the boat and propped them on the bench.

"Not some*thing,*" Townsend said, grim. "Some*one.*"

Shivers started in Glennon's gut and snuck outward to the tips of his fingers, flooding his body with fear. He peered down through the sea glass Gibraltar had stuck to the boat, through the wooden hull, through the night-blackened water and to the graves that existed below them. He imagined hands grasping at the boat, wrinkly and bloated with water, just like Townsend's.

And then, the boat jerked for a second time.

"It's not safe to sail during a storm," said a low, comforting voice from behind Glennon.

"Uncle Job!" Glennon cried, turning to find his uncle half in and half out of the water. He wore his ghost form, his body made of the tree that had killed him. The boat began to move once again, whatever had held it fast letting go as Uncle Job exerted pressure from behind.

"Job," Mom said from the front of the boat. The biggest smile Glennon had ever seen spread across her mouth.

"Ruby." Uncle Job continued to push the boat through the waves that splashed into the coast.

"What about your job?" Mom stayed turned toward Uncle Job. Glennon couldn't tell if the wet on her face was from tears or from Superior's waters.

"There may be consequences, but sometimes that's okay. Sometimes it's okay to take the risk."

Uncle Job walked forward and rested a hand made of twigs against Mom's shoulders. She looked into Uncle Job's face, her smile still in place. Glennon noticed then that Uncle Job wasn't the only new ghost who'd joined them. First Keeper Orwell and Second Keeper Ortez from Graving Lighthouse had joined them as well.

"We felt you break the light at Ingram. The whole isle felt you break the light. *We—*" Uncle Job gestured to the keepers beside him. "We couldn't figure out how to break the light at Graving on our own, but we could figure out how to leave and come here. We knew you would need help, and this much, we knew we could do."

"I've watched the living die for a century," said Second Keeper, and Glennon remembered how he'd blamed himself when the ship crashed on the cliff below Graving. *I should've started the foghorn sooner. This is my fault,* he'd said. "It's time to do something else."

"I've kept the records for two centuries," said the First Keeper, "but what other choice has there been? If we didn't keep the records, then who would?"

"We've acted as witness to the passing of lives." The Second Keeper hardly lifted his legs while he rode upon the waves. "But that no longer feels like enough. It's time we helped the living escape."

The First Keeper headed to the front of the boat. He raised his lantern above his head. Leading the way, he said, "If we get you far enough from Isle Philippeaux, you should be able to escape its grasp."

Hope filled Glennon. With all the ghosts present—Uncle Job and Keeper Orwell and Keeper Ortez and Keeper Delmont and Mr. Traxler and Townsend—it should be easy to sail away from Isle Philippeaux.

They could make it!

VOOMP. Air sucked across the boat. Glennon tipped out of his seat. He looked up, expecting to see Lake Superior opening wide her mouth and inhaling, but instead, he saw Everett hovering above the waves, a slight glow emanating from his frozen body.

"There's only one of you!" Lee shouted, almost standing up as she yelled. "One of you and *many* of us."

Townsend reached straight over Glennon's shoulder, her ghostly arm growing long. She grabbed the back of Lee's jacket, pulling her back onto her seat. "That's not true. You just can't see—"

Voomp. Voomp! VOOMP! Little bursts of wind cut across the lake. One by one, small puffs of light burst into existence, illuminating the fuzzy edges and strange innards of ghosts.

"Them," Townsend finished. "You couldn't see them."

There stood Miss Lacey with the lightning that ribboned along her skin. There was the man without eyes who'd scared Glennon and Lee. There was the postman and the grocery staff and sailors…so many sailors. Sailors wearing clothing that had to be from generations past, centuries when they didn't have Moon Boots or puffy neon coats. Behind all of them, ships came into view. The *Edmund Fitzgerald* with its rusting, ghostly body, and the *Anabeth* that Glennon had seen pinned to a rock.

And there, in the middle of it all, was Kit. Behind him,

stars speckled the night sky. They outlined the blurred lines of his ghostly body, little needles that seemed to pin him in place.

Glennon's heart fell and with it, went his body. He sank into Townsend's boat, huddling against the gemstones and tinfoil that riddled the sides.

32

Wind blasted across Lake Superior, whipped up by the ghosts before them. It peeled off their bodies and filled the air with fog. Glennon recognized the thick mists from the storm that had wrecked the *Anabeth*.

Beside Townsend's boat, the ghosts who sided with the living formed a circle, using their own energy to block the wind and fog from enveloping them. Uncle Job, with his body made from the sunken bones of a tree, swayed against the force of the wind, bending but not breaking. Standing steadfast.

I will protect you, said Uncle Job's love.

The storm worsened. Wind and sleet pummeled the outer ring the ghosts made, sending flurries of snow every which way, and beneath them, waves rose.

Glennon saw that Townsend no longer sat behind him working the motor. She'd joined the other ghosts in the circle around the boat, trying to protect them from the onslaught of the storm. He scrambled back and took up the handle to the motor, trying to mirror how he'd seen Townsend work the boat. As long as they headed away from Isle Philippeaux, they should be okay.

Glennon yelled, "Hold on!" and pressed the motor as fast as it could go. They shot across the lake, flying away from the island and the trap it'd set for them.

The ghosts kept up, flying along with them, paving the way, but one by one, they peeled off as ghosts in the opposing faction bombarded them. Mr. Traxler fought Miss Lacey. Keeper Delmont fought a keeper of another lighthouse. Townsend fought with Kit, lightning ripping open the sky above them. And as the ghosts around them veered away, the boat's protection disappeared.

Gales of wind ripped at them, and everyone ducked into the boat, trying to use its curved walls as protection. They traveled up one wave only to drop straight into the trough on the other side. Water poured in, swamping the bottom and drenching their pants. A ghost appeared directly in front of them on the lake. Water funneled inside it, a small vortex making up its surface—it must have died somehow by drowning, or by getting sucked into a swirling waterspout. It reached out for them.

Glennon threw the glass shard he'd taken from Ingram's light. Its shining surface reflected the light that spewed out of the ghost's body. The ghost covered its eyes with both arms and screamed, its moan of despair and sorrow filling the air, sluicing through the echoes of the wind. It dropped straight into the lake below.

Lee shouted. She held her own shard of glass high in the air, even as they raced along the waves, up one and down another.

Beside Glennon, Gibraltar flicked on a huge flashlight and shone it straight into the backside of Lee's glass. The light refracted, turning into a brilliant rainbow, but as the light cascaded around them, it highlighted a horrifying figure.

Everett.

Made entirely of the frozen ice that coated Superior midwinter, Everett stood directly before them. Waves billowed around him and freezing wind blew off his shoulders.

Glennon turned the boat, trying to go around Everett. They both spun sideways. Everett put down his head and used it like a battering ram, smashing his glacial skull straight into the hull. Everyone inside flew sideways with the force of the strike.

Glennon toppled out of his seat. His hip smashed into the side of the boat, and he tipped over its edge to plunge into the frigid water below.

33

The cold seized hold of Glennon's throat and shook loose the breath from his lungs. He gasped, sucking in water and struggling to swim *up*. His head popped out of Superior, even as his boots and coat grew heavy with water. The cold wrapped around his body, and his brain short-circuited.

Hands grabbed his and with a splash, he flew out of the lake. There, above him, stood Keeper Sanz, her terrible ghostly form lit with internal light. She plunked Glennon back down with his bottom nestled in the middle of a circular red and white life buoy that the keeper must have brought with her. His numb hands clung to the ring for dear life.

Keeper Sanz's face pressed close to Glennon's. Her breath scraped against his cheeks where water turned to ice on his skin, and the warm air from her ghostly lungs burned.

"*Help.*" Glennon struggled to speak.

"Did you find the truth of what haunts you?" Keeper Sanz said. "It's the only way to become free."

Glennon's eyelids froze closed, the water lining his lashes turning to ice. "I don't want to be haunted."

"We are all haunted, in some way." Keeper Sanz's hands brushed across his face, warm as the mug of tea she'd gifted him and warm as the heater he'd sat before. His insides thawed, the memory of drying inside her lighthouse filling his skin. "You get to decide how you will live. You get to decide who you will be. You get to decide to leave the haunting behind. Do you understand? You get to decide to leave all of this behind. You get to find a way to heal."

The ice on Glennon's skin melted. His eyes peeled open.

She grinned then, sudden and fierce, her mouth full of sharpened rocks. "But it is always, *always* good to ask for help when life spins out of your control."

Glennon sagged forward when Keeper Sanz's hands fell away. She rose before Glennon, tall as Spectre Lighthouse, her head blocking out the sight of the moon. When she tread over the water, her strides took her across Superior with ease. She headed straight into the center of the fray.

A small, mewling cry filled Glennon's ears. He searched the water for Seamus. Bobbing atop the water was Lee's backpack.

Panic filled Glennon and he glanced around for Lee even while he snatched the pack out of the water. He found Lee still in Townsend's boat. Everett hadn't smashed it into smithereens, but he had rent a massive crack up one side. Everyone clung to it, but it was fast filling with water. Uncle Job stood beside them, holding tight to the boat to keep it upright in the water.

Glennon unzipped the backpack, discovering Lee's Moon Boots had made her backpack float, and unzipped his coat. Seamus clawed out of the pack and straight onto Glennon's body, trying to climb onto his shoulders. Glennon tucked Seamus against his chest, now warm and dry thanks to Keeper Sanz.

He wrapped his coat around Seamus and zipped it back up, grateful for the first time that Mom always bought things oversized so he would have room to grow. He wrapped his arms around Seamus. Inside his coat, the cat's heart pounded, echoing each beat of fear that radiated through his own body.

Wind whispered around them. It sounded the same as the scratch of his dad's red pen across paper.

You need help, Glen, the wind said. *I can help you. Your mind has tricked you. You don't need to escape.*

You're making things up, Glennon almost told himself, but he was so tired of second-guessing his mind. It was exhausting in nearly the same way Superior's freezing waters were exhausting, sapping energy from his muscles and freezing his joints.

The wind kept speaking. *Things only seem bad because of the choice you're making. If you weren't trying to escape, the ghosts wouldn't have to try to stop you. No one would be hurt. You wouldn't be hurt. Your sister wouldn't be hurt. Your mother wouldn't be close to drowning.*

Glennon struggled to think. This moment was the same as in Townsend's ghost story, with the sailors hearing voices in the wind. He heard ghosts. He heard *Isle Philippeaux.*

He understood why Townsend's story had been so scary, why he'd been so terrified of the face that had appeared in the fire: Glennon had always lived inside a scary story, trapped beside a scary monster who had always tried to steal his life. Memories of his monster lived inside him. *Incompetent son* and *How useless are you?* And *Speak! You stupid child. How are you mine? No child of mine would be so incompetent,* and Glennon needing to apologize for every single thing about himself. *I'm sorry, I'm sorry, I'm sorry.*

He was so tired of apologizing for existing.

Glennon looked across the lake at his sister clinging to her seat. At his Mom, glittering in her shield of sequins. She'd opened her coat, and each small circle of light on her sequin jacket reflected the ghost that stood before her. *Kit* stood before her. Glennon couldn't hear what Kit said, but Mom spoke, and as she did, Kit listened. Glennon looked at Uncle Job, who used his body and strength to protect them instead of hurt them. He looked at each of the ghosts who were being whittled away as they fought Isle Philippeaux and the ghosts that were under its spell.

"I don't believe you, and I'm not going to stop fighting," he said to Isle Philippeaux, knowing it was listening. "If I stay here, I'll always be stuck. All I'll have is remembering, and I don't want to spend my whole existence remembering."

He understood how memories could live inside him. He knew how they could control him. He didn't want to be like the ghosts, forced to remember the way they'd died forever. He didn't want to live in the past.

"I want to *live*. If I stay, I'll have to hurt others. If I stay, I won't ever get to heal and feel better. I want to feel better and not always be scared."

He paused, trying to find the words to make Isle Philippeaux understand, and when he did, Everett appeared directly before him.

Glennon said, "I won't let you hurt me."

Everett's eyes—what appeared to be his eyes—seemed to blink inside his broken, slivered, icy body. "I'm stronger than you."

Glennon thought of his dad. He thought about what it meant to be *strong* and what it meant to be *weak*, and wondered why Isle Philippeaux had decided *it* was strong and *he* was weak.

He thought he understood why the ghosts hated their reflections. It must be terrible to look at yourself and only remember the way you'd died. It must be terrible to look at yourself and only think about how you would help hurt someone else. He thought that maybe people who made others miserable rarely wanted to look directly into their own pain. Maybe facing the truth made them question strength and weakness. Maybe it made them feel weak, and that's when they lashed out.

"It doesn't exist," Glennon said. "Isle Philippeaux doesn't exist."

"It's right there," said Everett, pointing behind him.

"It doesn't exist on any maps."

"That doesn't mean it's not *real*."

"It's real because everyone here thinks it's real. They give it power." Glennon tightened his hold on Seamus, taking comfort from the cat. "I don't want to give it power. I don't think it's real anymore."

Everett laughed, the sound harsh and grating—the same as ice cracking and sloughing apart.

You get to decide how you will live. You get to decide who you will be, Keeper Sanz had said. *You get to decide to leave the haunting behind.*

"I don't want to be haunted anymore," Glennon said.

"You can't decide not to be haunted!" Everett gestured to the island, to himself, to the ghosts behind him.

"I can too." Glennon knew healing from the ghosts would take time and work, but this was a start. This part, he could do fast. He could make Everett disappear and make the island disappear. He could save his family.

Everett's form shifted, little slivers of ice sticking out, pricking his body through with quills.

"Do you know why ghosts don't like their reflections?" Glennon watched Everett closely. "It's hard to look at the truth of who you are, especially if you don't like yourself or if you're haunted by who you are or by what you've done."

Glennon pointed down at Lake Superior. The water here had calmed ever since Keeper Sanz had walked by. His own face reflected back, along with Seamus's, whose fur fluffed under Glennon's chin.

"But I like myself," Glennon said. "I'm *choosing* to like myself right now. I choose to believe I'm smart, that I'm not useless or incompetent. I'm choosing to live and not get sucked back to the island."

Beside him, Everett tipped his head. His frosted, broken form rippled in the reflection in the black water.

"Why? Why would you do this?" Everett asked, staring at his ghostly body. "*I* was pulled here by another ghost. I was killed by someone else too. Why would you blame me? Why would you make me look at myself?"

Glennon glanced past Everett and at Isle Philippeaux. Eyes of light pricked the night: *on-off, on-off, on-on-off* went the rhythm of each of the lighthouses along the outer banks of the island, all except for Ingram. *Stay-here, stay-here, stay-stay-here,* they echoed inside Glennon's chest.

"I want to live," Glennon said to Isle Philippeaux.

Nothing. Happened. Isle Philippeaux gave no indication that it'd heard.

Glennon had thought that would be it. He thought defeating Everett lay somewhere in making Everett look at his reflection in the water, but instead of Everett disappearing into the depths of the lake, a voice shook over Superior's surface.

"I have to do everything myself, don't I."

Everett's expression turned from contemplative to horrified. His form fractured, flickering between his ghost and his human body. A rat crawled from inside his pocket and up onto his shoulder. Its white teeth shone against the moonlight above. Everett ducked his head and put up his arms, warding off the rat and reminding Glennon of the way he sometimes flinched back from his dad.

"I'm sorry," Everett whimpered. He hid his face with one hand and didn't look at the rat. "*I'm sorry.* I tried. Please don't punish me. Please, I'm sorry!"

Glennon felt Everett's horrified expression mirrored on his

own face, for the voice that had spoken from across the lake had been his dad's.

34

"I have to do everything myself." **Glennon's dad walked toward** his son from across the water.

This couldn't be happening—this wasn't possible! It wasn't possible that his dad was here, now. His dad was in Brussels!

Glennon couldn't quite see his dad from the distance, but he knew the way he stalked toward someone when he was angry. Swinging fists. Head thrown back. Stomping feet. A ghostly rope trailed behind him, connecting his body to the island. The farther he walked, the more Isle Philippeaux dimmed in the distance.

"I am surrounded by incompetence," Glennon's dad said.

He strode across the lake, each footfall shivering through Superior's surface. The ghosts around them stopped moving. They stopped fighting, frozen, seemingly no longer in control of their bodies or their powers. They each looked just as terrified of Glennon's dad as Glennon was.

Glennon's dad towered over him and the small life buoy

he sat in. He pulled up his pant legs a bit and crouched, so that he and Glennon were eye to eye. Fear wracked Glennon's spine, turning his body into a question mark, a half-formed moon, a slowly written G in cursive meant to match his dad's writing. It suffocated him.

"*Hello, Glen.*" His dad's voice trembled through Glennon, familiar and terrifying at once.

"You can't be here," Glennon whispered, weak.

"*Of course I'm here.*"

"I'm making you up. My brain is making you up because I'm scared. You're not real."

"*You have no idea what you're talking about,*" said his dad. "*Of course I'm real.*"

Fear flooded Glennon's brain. All the words inside him vanished, and his mind churned to a halt.

"*You always were a very sensitive boy. Sensitive and scared and stupid. But I forgive you. I'm here to help you.*"

Tears ran down Glennon's cheeks. He tried to wipe them away, but they froze in place.

"*It's alright, son. I forgive you for how you feel. I forgive you for disappointing me.*"

He heard the cadence of his dad's words, the way his dad's voice stayed low and calm. Once, when he was little, they took a road trip out to the country and they'd found a calf stuck in a wire fence. His dad had talked low and calm to the calf the whole time he'd worked to set the scared animal loose. That was the same way he talked to Glennon now.

"If you don't come home with me, what will your mom and your sister do? They can't leave me. You know they can't live without me."

Glennon smelled the soap his dad used, the one that came in a white box and always made him think of Sunday mornings when Mom made French toast and his dad took an early shower after going for a run.

"We have a good life together. I'm a good dad. I need each of you. You need *me."*

Glennon felt the press of a long hug before he went to bed, providing strength and comfort when he was scared of sleeping.

"It's your fault we're here, like this. It's your fault everyone's drowning and freezing and dying. If you hadn't left Isle Philippeaux, we wouldn't be like this."

Glennon's fingers slid against Seamus's fur. Seamus beamed his neon eyes straight at Glennon's dad and bristled in the way he did anytime his dad was around…anytime the island's ghosts or rats had come around.

"Leaving was very selfish of you. This is the good thing about being selfish though; you can always be better. You can work harder. You can become an improved version of yourself. You can return. You can come home to me."

Seamus shifted. He rustled something in an inner pocket of Glennon's jacket. Glennon dug it out and unfolded it: the tinfoil Gibraltar had given him. He flattened it on his lap and in its crinkled, wrinkly surface, he saw the true form of the thing before him.

The glowing, green eyes of dead rats peered out of his dad's face. His dad leaned close, and in the movement, the rats' skeletons clattered against one another. He saw the dead things of Isle Philippeaux—the flickering tails, the shifting ears, the whiskers and noses of the island's rats, all mixed together to form the curling shape of his dad's hair, the pointed nose on his face, the stubble that poked free of his chin.

This wasn't his dad. This was the *island*.

This was the thing that controlled all the ghosts, that took life and sucked it deep inside itself. The thing before him was made up of dead, stagnant things: birds and rats and fish. It was unchanging. It was endings and misery.

Everett had never controlled the rats. The rats had been Isle Philippeaux, and Isle Philippeaux had always controlled Everett. And too, it wasn't that monsters had lived in the mists of Isle Philippeaux, but that the monster *was* the mist. The monster *was* the isle, and it was standing right before him.

Glennon stared into Isle Philippeaux's face, even though it wore his dad's face like a costume or a suit. It might not actually *be* his dad, but still, it felt exactly like him—both good and scary at the same time. In some ways, Isle Philippeaux had been good—it had held Uncle Job and Townsend and Graving.

Why couldn't monsters be easy to hate?

"*You don't have a choice. It's time to come home, Glen.*" His dad spread his hands wide, and Glennon recoiled, his body pulling away automatically, even though his dad had never struck him before. "*This is all your fault. I haven't done anything to make you want to leave. I haven't done anything wrong.*"

The island was trying to convince him, because it thought Glennon would bend to his dad. But if his dad hadn't done anything wrong, then why did Glennon always feel like *everything* was wrong? Why had the entire world felt wrong while he was on the island…when he was with his dad?

"*I can see you're trying to think. You know you're not good at that—you're not smart enough. But that's okay. That's why you have me. I can be smart for you.*" His dad patted his chest, as if he was proud of being who he was. "*You're making things up, if you believe this situation is my fault, if you think you can leave.*"

But Glennon wasn't making things up. None of this was his fault. He was smart, and he was remembering things correctly. He remembered everything just fine. The truth was that while *he* was fine, his *dad* had not been fine. The island had not been fine.

He never should have been yelled at or called names. He never should have been made to feel stupid. He never should have been told that he couldn't speak or have emotions. He never should have been afraid, not in his home and not of his dad.

"*Glen—*"

With every bit of strength inside his body, even though it came out as little more than a whisper, he said, "My name is Glennon. I don't want to be called Glen. And I would like you to leave me alone."

"*It's time to come home.*"

"Leave me alone. I don't have to listen to you." Inside his pocket, he knew he would find a pair of bright purple earplugs. But he didn't need them. He could choose not to listen to the awful words the island spoke in his dad's voice

"*It's time to come home.*"

"You're what haunts me," Glennon said, finally knowing the answer to Keeper Sanz's question, *Did you find the truth of what haunts you?* He bent his head toward Seamus and inhaled the cat's wet kitty scent. He filled his senses with the warmth and safety of the animal tucked up against his heart.

"*It's time to come home.*"

And Glennon refused to listen or to answer. Isle Philippeaux and the costume it wore deserved nothing else from him. He wouldn't give anything else. Not one more word.

Not one more.

"IT'S TIME TO COME HOME!"

The roar that filled Glennon's ears contained a fury so great it tinged Glennon's vision red and black. The rampaging mass of rats that had pretended to be his dad all began squeaking at once, the noise of it filling Glennon's ears. Old instincts reared up in him. Who should he be right now? Happy Glennon or quiet Glennon or the Glennon who tried to be smart enough for his dad or the Glennon who knew how to stop himself from crying when he was being yelled at, because crying while being yelled at always made the yelling worse.

He knew, though, that he didn't need to be any particular Glennon. He could just be…*Glennon*. He could be himself. Being himself might not make his dad happy—nothing ever made his dad happy—but he could make *himself* happy.

He didn't respond to the island's summons to come home.

A whirl of wind flew by his ear, feeling exactly like a fist shooting past his head, and something heavy and thick punched into the water. A wave rose up to surround him. Glennon sucked in a breath and cupped his body around Seamus as Lake Superior enveloped them. The shock of its cold waters shriveled his lungs. He kicked and kicked his legs, straining to break the surface. And when he came up, his dad was no longer there. The island was no longer there, either.

The Waning had ended. Isle Philippeaux had disappeared. And Glennon, and his mom and sister and even Gibraltar, hadn't disappeared with it.

35

Warm hands picked up Glennon. Keeper Sanz cradled him tight, and immediately, Glennon and Seamus began to warm.

Glennon looked around to see that chaos no longer heaved at Superior's waters. The lake was calm and sweet, nothing of the monster it'd been moments before. All of the ghosts who had tried to drag them under had disappeared, and all those who were left were people who had helped save him. The living—Mom, Lee, Gibraltar. The dead—Uncle Job, Townsend, Mr. Traxler, Keeper Delmont, Keeper Orwell, Keeper Ortez, Keeper Sanz.

"The isle!" Townsend yelled. "It's gone!"

"*Ha!* The isle disappeared and didn't take us with it!" Keeper Sanz stretched her arms above her head and toward the stars.

Each of the ghosts collected around the living, Uncle Job going to Mom, and Keeper Delmont going to Gibraltar, and Townsend going to Lee. Slowly, Townsend's broken boat began to lift from the lake, water streaming out of it, as the ghosts held it aloft.

"What was it?" Lee asked. "What really was Isle Philippeaux?"

"Death," said Keeper Sanz. "Death and decay. After enough time, all of the lives lost on the lake added up. The death formed a sort of vortex. It became an island, and in the end, the island became conscious."

"Does it still exist?"

"Yes. Of course. I'm not sure there's a way to destroy it. The only thing to do is to escape and hope it doesn't return again."

"What did you do, Glennon?" Townsend asked. "I saw you talking to Everett, and then...everyone disappeared."

Glennon looked at Keeper Sanz, all of his words sticking tight in his throat. Embarrassment flooded him; he didn't *want* to talk. It felt uncertain and scary. He didn't want to tell anyone about the island looking like his dad.

"You said magic wasn't real," Glennon said to Keeper Sanz.

"Magic isn't real, but monsters are." She paused then added, "Any magic that exists in the world is the magic inside yourself. It's your strength and bravery. It's the love that's helped save you."

He glanced around the group and saw in their faces the sort of love each of them sent his way. *You are safe*, they all said. *You are strong, and you are brave.*

Taking a deep breath, he said, "Isle Philippeaux made itself look like my dad."

"I saw him too," said Lee. "I saw him walk up and crouch before you."

"I saw our dad," said Uncle Job.

"I saw both him and Hurley," whispered Mom.

"The isle looked like the bottom of the lake, to me," said Townsend.

"I saw my friends on the *Anabeth* dying," said Gibraltar.

The Second Keeper shook his head and said, "I saw the pirate who killed me."

"For me, the isle was the moment my husband died," said Keeper Sanz.

Isle Philippeaux had taken on different forms for everyone. They'd all seen what haunted them most. For Glennon, that had been his dad.

He said, "My dad talked to me. I…I didn't like it. He wasn't very nice and tried to make me feel bad. He tried to convince me to go back to the island." He brushed his fingers over the top of Seamus's head. "I didn't listen to him though. I told him to leave."

Mom said, "How?"

"I thought I deserved to feel safe. I wanted to be happy," Glennon said.

"It's not easy to be brave and move forward," said Keeper Sanz. "Change is difficult."

"Are we moving forward, then?" Townsend asked. "Is that why we didn't disappear along with the others?"

"It would appear that way," said Keeper Sanz.

"I believe, Townsend," said Mr. Traxler, "that when we decided to stop Ingram Lighthouse and help the living, that was us deciding to move forward and change as well."

"Isle Philippeaux had been haunting us, just as surely as ghosts have been haunting the living who've landed on the island," said Keeper Sanz.

"It's a good thing, not to be haunted," Townsend said. "At least it means we aren't stuck anymore."

"A very good choice," Keeper Sanz said. Warmth flooded from her body. Bits of her ghostly form shed off, dropping to sink into the water. "It will be good to move on."

Keeper Sanz sat Glennon down beside Lee in the boat.

"I've lived on that isle for a very long time," Keeper Sanz said in her softly lilting accent, her face tilted toward the sky. "When I was alive, the Lighthouse Service asked my husband and I to come to this country. Did you know that? My husband was so very good at his job, and they brought us across the ocean to work at a lighthouse in Duluth. He died at that lighthouse though. He fell off the roof, and I was left on my own, so I got a ticket on a ship, intending to cross the lake and make my way home. My ship went down in the middle of Superior, though, and so, instead of ending up at home, I ended up here, without my love. That's how I became a keeper in my own right, though I did so stubbornly. I had no desire for Isle Philippeaux to make use of me, even though it'd trapped me. I stayed in the lighthouse and refused to turn on the light because I didn't want anyone else to take my place."

First Keeper Orwell's dark skin glowed with the internal light of the ghosts. "My father was a paid servant at a lighthouse. He had just been freed from slavery. I learned the job from him."

Beside him, Keeper Sanz offered him her hand. He clasped it, and Glennon saw that bits of his ghostly form were evaporating as well. Both of them were fading, blending into the night.

First Keeper Orwell said, "I moved north to Michigan with my wife. I had children and grandchildren. Didn't expect to die on the lake during an ice storm, though I doubt anyone truly expects to die when they do. Isle Philippeaux needed a keeper at Graving, and I knew the duty well. I didn't want the living to join us, but I'd never heard of anyone escaping. It seemed the best I could do was to act as witness and record the lives of everyone lost."

"I was a sailor," said Second Keeper Ortez. He floated across the water, his legs not legs anymore so much as a dewy waterfall of droplets that hung suspended in the air. "It was a good job.

I made enough money during the spring, summer, and fall that I could live through the winter with my family in the city. But pirates tricked my captain and ran aground our ship. We were robbed, and our bodies were dumped in the middle of the lake. I had two babies. Little girls. I have no idea what became of them." Sadness dripped off his smile, and as he remembered the past, his gaze turned inward. "Orwell, you took me in. When I ended up stuck on the isle, you asked me to come and work as a keeper. I would have been lost without the offer."

First Keeper Orwell's shoulders looked a little less stooped than they had a moment before. He sighed, his breath fogging in the air and dimming the outline of his body just a little more. "I hope that whatever comes next, we both find our families."

Second Keeper Ortez smiled. He was nearly translucent.

"I died in a boating accident," Townsend said, quiet. Her face, revealed in full now with her hood tugged down and back, twisted. "Dad and I had taken out our row boat. We were supposed to stay along the shore, but winds rose up. We had no control. It was…"

"It was terrible," said Mr. Traxler. He appeared behind Townsend and wrapped his arms around his daughter. Then, he looked to Keeper Delmont. "But through it all, I found you."

"Even in death, there are beautiful, hopeful things," Keeper Delmont said, who set one hand on Mr. Traxler's shoulder. Both men disappeared a little, serene smiles covering their faces.

Glennon looked to Uncle Job. His uncle was slightly incorporeal as well. Glennon knew the others were leaving; was Uncle Job leaving as well?

Glennon, who was used to not having the right words at the ready, decided not to try to force himself to talk. He unzipped his coat farther and Seamus poked out his front paws and meowed. His rough tongue scratched Glennon's chin. Glennon was glad he had Seamus. He was glad he had his mom and Lee.

Into the silence and the night, they'd each let loose their truths, setting free the parts of them that had been haunted and full of sorrow and fear.

"We're free now, aren't we?" Townsend said. "Can we go? Can we leave this place?"

"Yes. It's time to leave," Keeper Sanz's voice, not louder than a whisper, filled the air, and then she was gone, drifting off toward the stars.

Each of the ghosts were carried away by the slight breeze that wafted over Lake Superior. The flotsam that had made up their bodies was released into her waters and the glowing, effervescent parts of them rose toward the sky.

"Thank you," said Townsend in Glennon's ear, and a moment later, she was gone, leaving only Uncle Job behind.

Townsend's boat floated and drifted, being pushed across the lake by Uncle Job.

"Where are we going?" Gibraltar asked after a while, breaking the silence.

"You'll see," Uncle Job said.

"I'm antsy to get home," said Gibraltar. He glanced over at Seamus. "I have a cat too, you know. An orange tabby. The animal shelter I got her from named her Fiona, but I call her Fifi. Sometimes when she meows, she sounds like a chirping bird."

"I'd like to meet her," said Glennon.

Pale, pink light crested the horizon, and when it did, they all realized Uncle Job had brought them to the ship whose crew had barely dodged crashing into Isle Philippeaux.

"Oye! Do you need a lift?" yelled a voice from the ship, a face appearing over the side. "You're welcome aboard our ship... that is, as long as you're not a ghost!"

36

A flurry of activity surrounded the living…and Uncle Job, though none of the crew on the *Lady Catherine* noticed him.

The crew had pulled them aboard *Lady Catherine* and had asked them their story, though truth be told, the men aboard the tug seemed less interested in listening and more interested in talking.

"It was a harrowing night," said one man. "A storm blew in all of a sudden."

"We saw the ghost ship," said another.

"*The Flying Dutchman,*" said the first. "It very nearly made us wreck!"

Glennon didn't tell them that not only were there ghost ships, but there was an entire ghost *island*.

The small ship was on its way to Thunder Bay, right near the border of Minnesota and Canada. Glennon honestly didn't care where they headed, just so long as they headed *away* from the mystery location of Isle Philippeaux.

After their small group was seen to, the crew mostly left them alone, except to supply them with warm, dry clothing and hot cocoa. Glennon tucked against Uncle Job's side and Uncle Job rested one arm over his shoulder. They watched dawn rise over the lake. He'd stood like this once, on the edge of the cliff near Graving, and used Uncle Job's body as protection. Now, Uncle Job was little more than a shadow at his side, fading as light spilled over Superior. Her waters shifted from black and angry to a sparkling sheen that reminded him of Townsend's bedazzled boat.

"I don't want you to go," Glennon said.

"Hmm." Uncle Job's voice rumbled, vibrating through Glennon's shoulder. "Should I tell you a ghost story?"

"I've had enough of ghost stories."

"*Listen.*" Uncle Job filled in his ghostly lungs with the crisp air of winter, and when he exhaled, fog coalesced before him. "Once upon a time, there was a man who became a ghost. Ghosts must, by definition, haunt something, and so, not wanting to bother anyone else, he haunted *himself*. It was a terrible existence, listening to the loud, angry thoughts inside his head, listening to the fear that made a home inside his body, watching the world pass him by. But what could he do? He was a *ghost*."

Glennon watched Uncle Job as he spoke. He peered up at

his chin, seeing through his whiskers and his jaw and his skull to the sky above with its puffy white clouds.

"Knowing you are a ghost and *admitting* you are a ghost are two very different things, and while he *knew* he was a ghost, he refused to admit it. Talking about things was…" Uncle Job stopped, seemingly unable to speak.

Glennon offered up a word: "Scary?"

"Yes, but more than scary. It's the same feeling as when someone raises their hand against you. It's the moment before they strike, when you know you could be hurt."

"*Vulnerable.* That's the word you're looking for," Mom said from Uncle Job's other side. "Talking about difficult things leaves you feeling vulnerable, as if someone might hurt you."

"Do you feel vulnerable?" Lee inched past Mom and snuggled up beneath Uncle Job's free arm.

Uncle Job looked down at Lee. "I do, but there is something comforting in being vulnerable with people I know who love me."

"What happened to the ghost?" Glennon asked, wanting to both know the end and *not* know the end at the same time.

Uncle Job said, "The end of the ghost story is that the ghost isn't a ghost any longer. He isn't haunted, because he learned to let go. He learned how to heal."

Glennon leaned against Uncle Job, trying to make his

2 9 6

uncle know that his love said, *I'm glad to have known you; thank you for being kind to me; I'm glad you're not haunted any longer.*

Uncle Job squeezed Glennon's shoulder and Glennon thought his love, in that moment, said, *I'm glad to have known you too; you'll be okay; you are good and smart exactly as you are.*

Uncle Job faded with the rising of the sun, and as he did, Glennon crept closer to his family. Gibraltar, too, stood beside them. They were bound together.

Glennon didn't know what would happen when they returned home, to their house that would still be empty of their dad. He didn't know how to ask Mom about his dad, but knew that tomorrow would come and with it, answers might come as well. And so too would the grief of losing Uncle Job.

For now, he had Mom and Leeunah and Gibraltar and Seamus. Seamus, who'd refused to climb out of Glennon's coat since they'd dried.

A warm breeze caressed the surface of Lake Superior. It tugged at Glennon's memories and made him wonder how he'd write about Isle Philippeaux and its ghosts, someday. He felt in his pocket for the papers he'd stuck there, after his backpack had dried on the deck of *Lady Catherine*. He imagined what sort of story he'd write later, what words he'd use.

That was the point, wasn't it? He could tell his story in any way he'd choose. He could write for himself and only for himself.

He'd once thought that what he most wanted was to be happy, but now he knew better. He wanted to be happy, but mostly, he wanted to be safe. And now, he was.

He was free.

LETTER TO THE READER

Dear Reader,

I want to explain that though this is a ghost story, it's also one that contains elements of abuse. The abuse Glennon suffers is, at times, very subtle. It might be difficult to pick out! Lots of times when people think of abuse, they think of people being physically hurt. This isn't what Glennon experiences. Rather, the abuse in his life is emotional and verbal.

We see inside of Glennon's memories the many times in which his dad used words like a knife to wound each of the members of his family and to create a very unsafe home. His dad is cruel with his words. He has taught Glennon to think very poorly of himself and not to believe his own thoughts or feelings. Their household is one that "walks on eggshells," with everyone being careful not to upset Glennon's dad or drive him toward anger. Their dad might never hit them, but he does throw and break objects in the house. He also screams and shouts, often doing so without any warning. This makes their home feel very unpredictable, like they could be yelled at any time for any reason. They are haunted by their dad's presence, whether or not he's actually there.

The effects of the abuse can be seen in how each of the family members has adapted to survive in their household. Both Glennon and Lee suffer from post-traumatic stress disorder (PTSD), while their mother has experienced depressive episodes.

When this book takes place (in the 1980s), we weren't as good at naming and describing mental illness. Now, we would be able to help Glennon identify the markers of PTSD he experiences: the way his brain stops working and he loses the ability to think clearly or speak, the way his body freezes when he senses someone might be angry, his need to try and be "perfect" so as not to upset his dad, and the way the past constantly overlaps with the present. We would help him understand that the reason he thinks awful things about himself (that he's stupid, irrational, shouldn't talk, and should never believe his emotions or his mind) is because he's been told these things by his dad. We would also be able to help Glennon understand that his intense need to protect his mother is tied to the danger they experience at home.

We would also be able to help Lee understand her anxiety. When she disappears at the beginning of the book into the coat closet and has trouble breathing, she is having a panic attack. It's her body's way of trying to protect itself during a time of high stress and fear. She has no control over this.

By the end of the book, Glennon's only just begun the process of healing. He's done the first step of realizing that something's wrong. He knows he deserves to feel safe at home and feel loved and protected by the adults in his life. I like to think that after this story, he goes on to have a happy and fulfilling life, as do Lee and their mother. They figure out how to heal, very likely with the help of a qualified therapist. The cycle of abuse stops, and none of them continue the pattern of abuse that their dad demonstrated (and also that their mom experienced with her own dad).

I hope that while you read this story that you didn't recognize any of Glennon's abuse in your own life or any of his symptoms inside yourself. If you did, though, trusted adults like teachers, guidance counselors, or school social workers can help.

Sincerely,
Juliana Brandt

ACKNOWLEDGMENTS

Whew! This book was a wild ride to create and bring to fruition. It was not easy to decide what form *Monsters in the Mist* should take, and I was only able to do so because of my support system.

An unending, heartfelt thank you to:

Natalie Lakosil, for always encouraging my concepts and being gentle in your feedback. Your thoughtfulness is always, always appreciated. Annie Berger, for being a phenomenal editor and knowing how to bring out the best in my writing. To the Sourcebooks staff who worked incredibly hard to complete this book: Chelsey Moler Ford, Zeina Elhanbaly, Ashley Holstrom, Maryn Arreguin, Pamela Seatter, Stephanie Rocha and Lynne Hartzer.

Cat Scully, for understanding how I was trying to tie together all of the themes in this story and for helping when I had no idea how to end the book. Also, you created the most gorgeous map! Thank you for sharing your talent. Lacee Little, I would be lost without you. You come along for the ride on every ridiculous book I write. Occasionally my doomsday mentality about writing gets the best of me, and you always know what to say to keep me in one piece; thank you for telling me I'm able to do difficult things. Ash Van Otterloo, for reading while I was drafting, when I doubted if I'd finish the story. Kurt Hartwig, for always seeming to understand what I'm trying to write before I do. Your ability to hone in on what I'm trying to say through my writing is, at times, otherworldly. Rebecca Petruck, for encouraging me to rest; your support from afar has shored up my emotional reserves more times than I can count. Mary Parton, for reading the first draft and telling me I was on the right track. Mary Roach, for knowing exactly who my characters were. Kristen Kearns, for helping me understand what it means to heal. Bronwyn Deaver, for feedback that was transforming, both for me and for this book. Jessica Vitalis, for giving me clear eyes; your help served as a rescue mission in the last minutes. My sensitivity readers, this book would never have been published without you. Thank you for lending your wisdom. Lauren Spieller, I couldn't dedicate this book to you, because I dedicated it to my parents, but here you go: A massive thank you for helping me solve the ending of *A Wilder Magic*.

Lucas Werner, you show me the sort of love that says, *I will always give you kindness*. I couldn't have gifted Glennon the sorts of love that healed him without knowing you.

My sister, Katie, who has always been like Lee, ready to listen and support. Doing "the work" is not easy, but it's easier with you around.

My dad, Randy. How lucky is it that I have a dad who's always excited to brainstorm new story ideas and magic systems? Do you remember hiking and talking about ghosts that appeared in beams of lighthouses? Thank you for always encouraging creativity and being a key part of my writing process.

My mom, Marsha. Writing this book during a pandemic and during a difficult teaching year was not easy, but I was able to do it because you always taught me how to take care of my heart. Thank you.

To both my parents: You made "home" synonymous with "safety." Thank you for always making home be a place of refuse.

ABOUT THE AUTHOR

Juliana Brandt is an author and kindergarten teacher with a passion for storytelling that guides her in both of her jobs. She lives in her childhood home of Minnesota, and her writing is heavily influenced by her travels around the country and a decade of living in the South. When not working, she is usually exploring the great outdoors. She is also the author of *The Wolf of Cape Fen* and *A Wilder Magic.*. Find her online at julianalbrandt.com.